FLYNN'S
IN

Novels by Gregory Mcdonald:

Running Scared
Love Among the Mashed Potatoes (Dear M.E.)
Fletch and The Widow Bradley
Fletch
Carioca Fletch
Confess, Fletch
Fletch's Fortune
Fletch's Moxie
Fletch and The Man Who
Who Took Toby Rinaldi?
Flynn
The Buck Passes Flynn
Flynn's In

Chess game courtesy of Abraham J. Bradley,
Shrewsbury, Massachusetts, U.S.A.

FLYNN'S IN

by

Gregory Mcdonald

THE MYSTERIOUS PRESS

New York

Text Design by Denise Schultheis at the Angelica Design
Group Ltd.

Jacket illustration copyright © 1983 by Bob Walker

Library of Congress Catalogue Number: 83-63161
ISBN: 0-89296-085-X TRADE EDITION
ISBN: 0-89296-086-8 LIMITED EDITION

FIRST EDITION

To Jane Choate Swan

FLYNN'S IN

Flynn answered the telephone saying, "I'll tell him when he comes in."

The upper corridor was lit only by the dim safety lights on the stairs leading down to the front hall.

"This is Eddy D'Esopo, Frank."

"Is it, indeed?" Flynn's hearing was so acute that having once heard a voice usually he could identify it immediately. "You don't sound like yourself at all."

"There's been some trouble," the Commissioner of Boston Police said.

"Not personal, I hope. Are you all right?"

"I don't like getting you into this, Frank. I don't know what else to do. The matter has to be investigated. Your prestige...I mean, you'll be believed, no matter what you say."

Flynn heard that none of his children was stirring.

"Anyway, that's what we've decided." The Commissioner sighed.

"What time is it, anyway?" Flynn's watch was on his bedside table.

"Quarter past two. Something has happened that shouldn't have."

"Isn't that just the way?"

"It will take some understanding on your part, Frank. Some discretion." The Commissioner hesitated while Flynn discreetly said nothing. "Anyone else I can think of...Well, I'd hate to think how anyone else might use this situation. It could become a dog and pony show very easily."

"Commissioner," said Boston Police Inspector Francis Xavier Flynn, "if this conversation has a topic, don't you think we both ought to know what it is?"

"What? Oh."

Flynn seldom raised his very soft voice. "What are you talking about, man?"

"I want you to come here. Where I am. Immediately. Do you have gas in your car?"

"Probably."

"You'll need gas. Do you have a pencil and paper? The directions are sort of complicated."

Flynn's bare feet were getting cold. "Hold on," he said. "I'll go to a phone downstairs."

On the kitchen floor, Flynn's bare feet became even colder. "I have paper," he said into the wall phone. On the other side of the paper was Elsbeth's shopping list. He noticed broccoli was listed. "I have a pen. Where am I going?"

Slowly, deliberately, the Commissioner gave Flynn directions. At first Flynn would be on highways, then on byways distinguished by route numbers, then on roads he would have to navigate by noticing the occasional church steeple, gas station, silo, finally on what was described as a timber lane. Flynn filled the whole side of the piece of paper with directions.

"A bit outside my jurisdiction," Flynn said. "Yours, too."

"It's a rod-and-gun club," Eddy D'Esopo said.

"It's outside the limits of the City of Boston," Flynn said.

"Yes. It is."

"It isn't even in this state," insisted Flynn.

"No," the Commissioner agreed. "It isn't."

"Good Lord, man, I have to ask: Do you know what you're doing? Not all the decisions we make this hour of the night are the best."

"Come alone. Tell no one where you're going. Not even Elsbeth."

"Commissioner, what are you getting me into?"

"You have experience, Frank, handling big matters. Affairs of state. I think you do. I mean, you didn't come up through the ranks. You came to us from Washington, or Zurich, or someplace. You'll know how to handle this."

"Commissioner, at the moment I'm trying to handle this case of vehicular homicide that happened last night, this hit-and-run situation of the bicyclist on Tremont Street."

4

"Sergeant Whelan can carry on for you, Frank. He's a big boy now."

"Grover," grumbled Flynn. "I'm personally interested in this investigation."

"You can direct Sergeant Whelan by telephone, Frank. From here. You know you can."

"Direct Grover! I can't make Grover go in the right direction in an elevator in the basement!"

"I'll phone headquarters in the morning and get your desk cleared for you."

"Wednesday I'm supposed to testify at that trial of the man who rigged the furnace in his partner's house to blow up. Nasty parcel he is."

"Grover—I mean, Sergeant Whelan can testify for you. Your notes must be in your office."

"With Grover testifying, the prosecutor will go to prison, the judge will go insane, and the defendant will go to Acapulco."

What Flynn was not mentioning was that the next afternoon he was to try the Mozart piece *ensemble* with his children. They had been practicing it three weeks.

"I'll be waiting up for you, Frank. Tell no one where you're going."

The telephone line hummed.

At the kitchen table, Flynn turned the piece of paper over and did his children a favor. He crossed broccoli off the shopping list.

He then hung up the kitchen phone, put the kettle on to boil, went upstairs, hung up that phone, and awoke his wife.

He told her everything the Commissioner said, including that he wasn't to tell her. While he was dressing, she copied out the driving directions for him on another sheet of paper so she could keep her shopping list. She didn't notice the list had been emended.

In the kitchen, while she was making a bacon sandwich for him to have with his tea, he telephoned his office in The Old Records Building on Craigie Lane and asked Detective Lieutenant Walter (Cocky) Concannon (Retired) if he'd like to join Flynn for a few days in the country.

5

Cocky said he thought that would be nice; he'd like very much to accompany Flynn.

"I'm Flynn," he said through the car window to the large man carrying a rifle and a flashlight.

As soon as the headlights of Flynn's ancient Country Squire station wagon had made visible the tall chain-link fence across the lumber road, this bulky man had stepped out of the mist from a dark shed.

"What have we here?" Flynn had said to Cocky. "Not girls in long tresses bidding us welcome, I think."

The guard had signaled Flynn to roll down his window.

He flashed his five-battery light at the two men in the car.

"You're supposed to be alone," the guard said.

"I am alone," said Flynn, "except for my friend."

In the very first light of dawn, minute drops of mist stood out on the guard's rough lumber jacket. The jacket bulged over his right hip.

Keeping the beam of the flashlight inside the car but not in their faces, the guard asked, "Identifications?"

Flynn took his card from the Winthrop Public Library out of his wallet and handed it to the guard. Cocky handed over his Social Security card.

The guard looked at the two cards in his hand an uncommonly long time. "Francis Xavier Flynn," he said. A drop of water from the man's hat landed on Flynn's library card. "Walter Concannon."

"Boston Police Detective Walter Concannon, Retired," said Flynn.

"I'll have to call the house."

"Tell them to put on the tea water," said Flynn. "I trust getting here hasn't been half the fun."

The guard lumbered toward the shed and entered it. A light went on in the shed.

Flynn looked at Cocky. "You're not welcome," he said.

He turned off the motor.

7

Inspector Francis Xavier Flynn and Detective Lieutenant Walter Concannon had first met at Cocky's retirement party. Cocky's retirement was early by years. His retirement party took place the first Friday night after he had been released from the hospital.

While reading counterfeiter Simon Lipton his rights, in the living room of Lipton's home, preparatory to arresting him, Detective Lieutenant Walter Concannon had been shot in the spine by Simon Lipton's nine-year-old son, Petey.

Simon Lipton was convicted of counterfeiting and imprisoned. Petey was sent to a diagnostic home for a month, and then released into the custody of his mother.

After months in the hospital, Detective Lieutenant Walter Concannon, permanently partially paralyzed on his left side, was retired, disabled, on half pay.

The Police Department threw away the contents with the wrappings.

At the retirement party, Flynn and Cocky discovered their mutual enthusiasm for chess.

The morning after the retirement party, while Flynn worked at his desk in his office in The Old Records Building on Craigie Lane, Cocky entered without knocking and without speaking. In his right hand he carried a hand-tooled chess set and board.

While Flynn watched wordlessly, Cocky cleared a side table by the unused fireplace, laid out the board and set out the chessmen.

And left.

A half hour later he returned with a tray in his right hand, with two mugs of tea on it. He placed one mug of tea on the white side of the chessboard, the other on the black side. He pushed two dusty chairs that were being stored in a corner of the office into place at the table, sat in one, and moved a white pawn.

He then sat back and looked at Flynn sitting with his back to the huge arched window.

The right side of Cocky's face smiled.

Flynn assumed Cocky had given up whatever his domestic

8

arrangements were when he was retired and appropriated a closet or whatever in the tomb-like Old Records Building. (Only the front half of the first floor was used as a police station; the surrounding neighborhood generally had been abandoned by its residents. The rest of the building was used for Police Department storage, that is, as a bureaucracy's wastebasket. The rear of the second floor was Flynn's office, enjoying grand architectural dimensions and style but no housekeeping whatsoever.)

Flynn never asked Cocky if he had moved into the building. He knew Cocky had no family, except for an old cousin in Nahant. On half pay, Cocky could afford little. Flynn knew he was not the only one to sleep on the nine-foot leather couch in his office. Any time of the day or the night Flynn called his office, Cocky answered.

Besides answering the telephone, Cocky did what typing and filing obviously needed doing, slowly and laboriously (he had learned neither skill), pretty much limited to the use of his right hand. He made himself useful. He soon proved himself a wizard at research. Any question that Flynn asked the air Cocky had an answer to in a fraction of the time paid researchers would have spent, even using computers. Cocky researched questions no one thought of asking. And once on the trail of a fact, Cocky was as relentless as a hound under a full moon.

And at the table next to the drafty fireplace, many cups of tea were consumed, many games of chess were played.

So Cocky was waiting on the Craigie Lane curb when Flynn arrived in the car at three o'clock in the morning. Flynn smiled when he saw him. Cocky had never accepted an invitation for lunch outside the office, for dinner or the odd musicale at Flynn's home. He had never even offered an excuse; just the simple, "No, thanks, Inspector." And here he was waiting on the curb at three o'clock in the morning, his old Boston Police satchel, doubtlessly now carrying a few clean shirts, etc., razor, toothbrush, dangling from his right hand, a portable chess set tucked under his arm.

Together they drove in Flynn's boxy Country Squire through the long course of directions to a rod-and-gun club. They spoke to each other hardly at all.

9

Cocky did not ask where they were going in the middle of the night, or why. Flynn wondered what Cocky had inferred from the strange invitation. He wondered why Cocky had accepted. Astutely, Cocky looked for the landmarks and read off the directions. Even in the fog and drizzle he seemed to enjoy the ride.

The light in the shed went off.

The guard, still carrying his rifle, sauntered back across the hard ground toward them.

Flynn rolled down the window again.

The guard handed Flynn's library card and Cocky's Social Security card back to Flynn. "You can go up," he said. "Just follow the road. You can't go wrong."

He went in front of the car and swung open the right half of the fence gate.

"It seems you've been accepted, Cocky." Flynn rolled the window up and started the engine. "You have an Irishman's invitation. You haven't been told to go away."

The dirt road climbed into dawn light, fell into fog patches, twisted and turned among huge gray rocks and tall, dark, heavy, dripping pine trees. On the last knoll they saw a lake shimmering flat and gray ahead of them to their left.

They came to the lake and went kilometers along the curve of it.

And then before them, beside the lake, up from it half a kilometer, sprawled a large, dark-timbered lodge. Its original center was three stories high, its long wings two. Asymmetrically, graystone chimneys rose above the brown-green roofs. The windows were small and, except for four in the center, unlit. A deep veranda studded with rocking chairs ran along all sides of the building visible from the front. Between the building and the wooden docks on the lake sloped a yellowing lawn.

"My God," Flynn said. "It's a bonfire awaiting a match."

To their right was an unpaved car-park. Two of the dozen cars in it were limousines. A third was a Rolls Royce sedan. A fourth was a Porsche. There were three Mercedes, two BMWs, and three Cadillacs. The license plates were of various surrounding states.

10

"Where are we?" asked Flynn. He parked his station wagon far from the herd of gleaming steel and chrome. "At a hairdressers' convention, I wonder?"

He locked his car.

A dark Lincoln Continental, with driver, was waiting outside the front door.

As Flynn and Cocky were reaching the steps leading up to the veranda, a large distinguished-looking man in a gray suit came through the front door and headed for the car. He gave them a friendly nod.

After the man had gotten into the front passenger seat of the Lincoln and closed the door, Cocky said of him, "That's Governor Caxton Wheeler."

"Is it indeed?"

The Lincoln did move, but so slowly its forward progress was hardly noticeable. It was being driven over the slightly uneven dirt driveway surface as if it carried uncrated eggs.

Cocky said, "They say that one day Caxton Wheeler is going to run for The White House."

On the front steps the two stared at the car. It was going around the grassy circle at a pace so slow as to make any turtle yawn before getting out of its way.

"Well," commented Flynn. "He'll never get there at that rate!"

11

3

"**F**or God's sake, Flynn." Commissioner Eddy D'Esopo stood by the huge, lit fieldstone fireplace in the main hall of the Rod and Gun Clubhouse. His eyes flickered at Cocky Concannon, who had trailed Flynn through the door.

"Here we are," said Flynn.

D'Esopo glanced at the white-coated butler who had let them in, then glared at Flynn. "There was to be no 'we,' Frank."

"Would you like some coffee, sir?" the butler asked Flynn. "Before we settle you in?"

Flynn pulled a bag of herbal tea from his jacket pocket and dangled it in the air. "If you'd surround this with hot water, we'd be most grateful."

The butler chuckled and took the tea bag. He was a short man, compactly built. Muscles bulged the shoulders and sleeves of his white jacket.

Flynn held up two fingers. "Two cups, please. One for me. One for my friend, who is known to favor the flavor of Red Zinger in dawn's early light."

The butler held Flynn's attention. "Lemon, sugar, cream?"

"Naked," said Flynn. "As naked a cup of tea as you ever set to steep."

"Red Zinger," Commissioner Eddy D'Esopo muttered into the fireplace.

"My name is Taylor, sir," the butler said. "If there is anything I can do for you and your friend to help make you comfortable, please let me know. Unfortunately, breakfast is not prepared until eight o'clock."

"Taylor, is it?" said Flynn. "Butlers are named Taylor, and tailors are named Vanderbilt. Who says the world doesn't progress?"

Still grinning, the butler left through a small door at the side of the fireplace.

"Well, Cocky," Flynn said. "At least the butler named Taylor doesn't mind seeing you."

Against the wall the other side of the fireplace was a large bar table. Bottles of all the best brands of liquor were standing free. There was a tray of various-sized glasses on the table, as well as a large silver ice bucket. Condensation on the bucket indicated it was filled with ice even at that hour.

Flynn looked around the cavernous room, at the Native American woven rugs on the dark gleaming, wide-board floors, the red leather chairs and couches, the massive mahogany tables, the deer and moose heads, trout and bass plaqued and mounted on the walls. He rubbed his hands together. "Just like home," he said in his soft voice. "Except most of the heads in my living room are still breathing."

He dropped himself into a massive leather chair near the fireplace.

"What's what's-his-name doing here?" D'Esopo said quietly, tightly into the fireplace.

The Commissioner was almost as big a man as Flynn, which was very big indeed. Whereas Flynn's head was peculiarly small for his body, D'Esopo's double chin and increasing baldness made his head seem almost too large. Too many administrative lunches and politic dinners had caused the Commissioner's waist to swell below his huge chest.

Softly, Flynn said, "Commissioner, you do remember Detective Lieutenant Walter Concannon, don't you? Been retired for some time now."

The retired Detective Lieutenant stood in the middle of the room looking like a very small island far out in a very big sea.

"Of course." The Commissioner sighed. He turned from the fire and approached Cocky with his hand out. "How are you, Walter?"

"Fine, thank you, Commissioner."

"I hear you've been a great friend to our unorthodox Inspector Flynn. Solve all his cases for him without moving a muscle."

Then the Commissioner glanced at Cocky's left side and winced at his own tactlessness. "Forgive me. It's early in the morning. I haven't slept much."

13

Cocky smiled as much as he could. "Without moving half my muscles, Commissioner. You have me on half pay."

"He uses all his very considerable brain," said Flynn. "For which he's not paid at all."

D'Esopo looked from Cocky to Flynn.

"Cocky's enforced retirement," Flynn continued quietly, "is a discouraging testament to the value the Boston Police Department places on brains."

After digesting this apparent digression, D'Esopo said to Cocky: "Frank was supposed to come alone, Walter. He couldn't have heard me."

"Sure I heard you," Flynn said from his chair. "Have I ever not heard anything, to my infernal regret? Now, charitably, I am giving you a chance to see. Whatever it is I'm to do here, I mean to let you see up close that I'll do it the better with the able assistance of Detective Lieutenant Walter Concannon." Then Flynn added: "Retired."

"Always the personal angle, Frank," D'Esopo muttered. "Always reforming the world."

"Sure," said Flynn. "It's part of my charm, it is. Can't have part of me, you know, without acceptin' the whole man. That's what needs sayin' here."

"Walter," D'Esopo said. "I don't blame you for coming. I'm sure you're an innocent victim of Flynn's relentless idealism."

"Well said," said Flynn. "And true."

D'Esopo returned to the fireplace. "But, Frank, I'm not sure you and I are going to survive this intact. That's what needs sayin' here. No matter what your motives, I doubt you've done Walter a favor by bringing him along."

"That bad, is it?"

Taylor entered with two cups of tea on a tray. D'Esopo fell silent.

"Some sort of a private club, is this?" asked Flynn.

"Yes," D'Esopo said.

"For hunting and fishing? Bringing to halt the beasts that run and swim?"

"Hunting and fishing," D'Esopo said.

Cocky took his cup without the saucer.

14

"And does it have a name," asked Flynn, "other than The Rod and Gun Club?"

"It's called The Rod and Gun Club," said D'Esopo.

"Not a name designed to attract much attention." Flynn took his own cup of tea. "Sure, you wouldn't see the signs leading to it unless you knew they were there. Very big, is it?"

"Two thousand acres," said D'Esopo.

"Two thousand acres!" marveled Flynn, settling back with his tea. "Some spots on this earth calling themselves countries aren't as big as that!" He sipped tea. "And tell me: does the chain-link fence, four meters high, with barbed wire on top run around the whole two thousand acres?"

"It does," said D'Esopo.

"And is it for keeping the beasts of prey inside, or those who would pry outside?"

Across the room, Taylor had stopped to straighten some magazines on a table. Under the tall table lamp he was taking a long look at Flynn.

"I guess it does both," said D'Esopo.

"Many members?" enquired Flynn.

"I don't know how many members, Frank. Do you?" he asked the butler.

"No, sir."

"I'm not a member," D'Esopo said. "I was invited here for the weekend."

Cocky had replaced his empty cup on the tray Taylor had left on a reading table. Dragging his left foot behind him, he was floating around the room with apparent aimlessness.

"Cocky," Flynn said. "You're a guest of a guest of a guest. Delicate standing indeed. We'd better plan to make our own beds."

Picking up the tray, Taylor laughed out loud.

"Cocky identified Governor Caxton Wheeler leavin' as we were arrivin'," said Flynn.

"Did he?" asked D'Esopo indifferently.

"Cocky tells me the man is being mentioned as a possible presidential candidate."

D'Esopo shrugged. "Anything's possible — as you love to say."

15

Taylor left the room.

Flynn finished his tea.

"Eddy," he asked. "Why am I here?"

"There's been an accident, Frank."

"Ach!" said Flynn. "Almost thirty years on the police force, and the man uses a euphemism like that! Why don't you just tell me, man, who did what to whom?"

D'Esopo hesitated. "It's possible someone shot himself while cleaning his shotgun."

Flynn put on a surprised face. "A shotgun! What a mistake! Even someone who's never seen a shotgun before knows instantly whether it's loaded."

D'Esopo said nothing.

"For that matter, Eddy," Flynn asked gently, "after almost thirty years on the police yourself, if an investigation is needed, why aren't you investigating it yourself?"

"I wouldn't." D'Esopo took a moment to organize his thoughts. "Twenty-seven years on the police force. Right, Frank. But I started as a rookie on the beat. Came up through the ranks. I have a Ph.D. I got it at Northeastern University night school. Frankly, I, uh....My wife has a large family. Spread throughout the city. With some political enthusiasm. They've been able to do the right things, over the years, without my, uh—"

"—having to commit or compromise yourself," Flynn finished for him.

"I know cops, Frank. I know crooks. I know a certain level of politicians. I've been invited to The Harvard Club and the Algonquin Club a few times..."

"Nothing like this place, you're saying."

"I don't know these people, Frank."

"They intimidate you."

"I've never been given your full dossier, Frank. Sergeant Whelan has passed around scuttlebutt about your mysterious meetings at Hanscom Airbase, and other places."

"Ah, Grover," mourned Flynn. "If that man had a brain instead of a mouth, the world would be better served."

"How many times is it now I've given permission to have

16

you pulled off everything while you disappeared God-knows-where to do God-knows-what for God-knows-who? It always goes in the record that you're off with an attack of appendicitis or colitis, and I always sign it. How many times have you had your appendix removed, Frank?"

"Let me count the scars."

"My suspicion is you're not off hosing down the ordinary, garden-variety crook."

"Eddy," said Flynn. "Your speech is becoming colorful."

"Exactly," said the Commissioner. "Mostly what I do these days is sign personnel excuses and give after-dinner speeches about our fully dedicated men in blue."

There was a rattle and stomping from the front hall. A man's voice said, "Never saw such perfect light. Full creels an hour before breakfast. I wonder if it's some sort of record?"

"I doubt it," said another voice.

D'Esopo stopped talking.

Two men in fishing gear and stockinged feet entered the room. They looked surprised in seeing men in the room they did not know.

Cocky glanced at Flynn in surprise.

One of the men Flynn faintly recognized. He had seen pictures of him in the newspaper, on the television.

"Good morning," the man said.

"Good morning," answered D'Esopo.

"Ring for Taylor, will you?" one man said to the other. He came across the room to the bar table and poured himself three fingers of Wild Turkey bourbon.

He downed it in a swallow. "They were really biting," he said to the room at large.

After pressing a wall button, the other man went to the bar table. They each made themselves taller drinks, with bourbon, ice and water.

Taylor came through the small door by the other side of the fireplace.

"Taylor," one of the men said. "Our creels and boots are in the front hall. You'll find them full."

"Both the creels and the boots!" laughed the other man.

17

"Full creels. But ol' Hewitt sure isn't the man he used to be."

Taylor acknowledged their wishes, then said to Commissioner D'Esopo, "Mister Rutledge has heard Mister Flynn is here. He'd like you both to go up, now."

"All right." D'Esopo moved a little too fast halfway across the room. He looked back to see why Flynn wasn't following.

Slowly Flynn rose from the comfortable chair by the fire. He crossed the room to Cocky and took him by the left elbow.

He walked Cocky into the front hall.

From a few steps up the wide, wooden staircase carpeted in forest green, D'Esopo said, "Frank. This doesn't include Walter. Just you and me, please."

"Just having a quiet word with the retired one, Eddy. I'll be right along."

Flynn turned his back to the stairs and asked Cocky quietly, "Who are those two men?"

"One is Senator Dunn Roberts." Cocky did not seem surprised at Flynn's not recognizing a United States Senator. He gave Flynn the Senator's party affiliation and state.

"And the other one?" asked Flynn.

"I'm pretty sure it's Walter March. You don't see too many photographs of him."

"And who's he when he's at home?"

"He owns a lot of newspapers."

"A powerful man, would you say?"

"Very."

"Oh," said Flynn. "I see. I think I'm beginning to see." Flynn asked Cocky one more question: "What's a Rutledge?"

"There is a Charles Rutledge," Cocky answered. "Any utilities he doesn't own, he's on the boards of. He's an art collector. Also, I believe, through his wife he invests in theater."

"Cocky." Flynn started up the stairs. "You're worth your weight in lobster tails."

4

"**C**harles Rutledge the Second." The man in the dressing gown announced his name as if stating a universal certainty, such as, *The East is where we say the sun rises.* In shaking hands with Flynn he did not smile. His eyes, cold for brown, beamed into Flynn's only long enough to tell him that Flynn never, ever would surprise him. "My assistant, Paul Wahler."

The other man in the room was dressed in a full, three-piece dark suit, necktie, black city shoes. His smile, when he shook hands with Flynn, looked as if it came from a box. In his left hand was a manila folder.

Outside was full daylight, however gray and overcast. The dark morning and the small windows required the lights to be lit in the small living room of Suite 23. The chairs and divan in the room were patterned in large, bright flower blossoms. Through a partially opened door, Flynn saw an unmade bed.

"I've telephoned some of the others," Rutledge said to Commissioner D'Esopo. "They concur in our decision, and advise us to go forward as planned." To everyone, he said, "Do sit down."

The four men sat on the blossoms. Rutledge took the chair with his back to the window light.

"At The Rod and Gun Club, tradition is that we dispense with titles and ranks, Flynn."

"Very democratic, I'm sure," said Flynn.

"How much has D'Esopo told you?"

"He's been as quiet as a Chihuahua in a snowstorm."

"I'd like to meet with you twice this morning, if you don't mind," Rutledge said. "I want to meet with you now to stress the delicacy of this matter. After your—shall we say?—discreet preliminary investigations, I'd like to meet with you again. Say about ten o'clock. That should give you time to view the body and have a good breakfast."

"And whose body am I viewing," asked Flynn, "before the toast and marmalade?"

"Oh, we can provide you with a better breakfast than that," smiled Rutledge. "The body is of Dwight Huttenbach." Rutledge waited futilely for Flynn's reaction. "You don't know who he was?"

"Already having an impression of your membership," answered Flynn, "I would suppose he was a barber keen on huntin' and fishin'."

Rutledge's smile assured Flynn Rutledge was not surprised. "United States Congressman Dwight Huttenbach." He mentioned Huttenbach's congressional district, state and party affiliation. Neither the state nor the party affiliation matched the state or the party affiliation of the United States Senator downstairs sipping a preprandial bourbon.

"By the way," Rutledge added, to D'Esopo. "I've talked with his wife. Mrs Huttenbach. First name . . ."

"Carol," said Wahler.

"Seems to be taking it as well as can be expected. She's on her way up. To Timberbreak, that is."

"I see," said D'Esopo.

Flynn noticed slight perspiration on D'Esopo's face. Even in his tweed suit, Flynn was surely not warm enough to perspire.

Rutledge said to Flynn: "The Congressman was killed by a shotgun blast."

" 'Was killed,' " echoed Flynn. "I see you're not givin' me the accidental euphemism."

Rutledge opened the palms of his hands to Flynn. "I'm not a policeman, Flynn. I have no expertise in such matters. You need to go see what is to be seen. I've asked Wahler to drive you."

Instantly, Wahler stood up to go.

Looking at Rutledge's silhouette against the window, Flynn said, "Usually people rush to show the police the corpse. Seldom are we invited in, given tea and, in a word, read our rights."

"You brought a man with you, Flynn."

"My driver."

"I'd like you to vouch for his discretion."

"You mean, his silence?"

"This is a delicate matter, Flynn," Rutledge said most

20

reasonably. "Huttenbach was young, with a wife and children. Other family. He represented an important constituency. He was enormously popular, greatly respected. A young man with a great future in national politics. I believe it important not to nullify such a man in death. Don't you? Don't you think it important not to break people's hearts?"

A week before, also at dawn, Flynn had arrived at a city housing project. A man had been stabbed to death by his wife. They had eight children. People from the project were stirring around in various sleep apparel, barefooted for the most part, crying, screaming, shouting things that were not understandable. Broken hearts were all over the sidewalk and the stairs. Most of the eight children were huddled in a corner of the open kitchen, like so many wide-eyed, trembling mice in a trap. One fat daughter sat on a bed watching cartoons on color television. The man had been nullified — as had his wife.

"Something terrible has happened," Rutledge said. "I'm sure you agree with me it's important, for all concerned, that the right face be put on it."

Flynn looked at Rutledge's silhouette another long moment.

Then, without saying anything, he stood up from his chair.

Wahler had opened the door to the corridor and awaited Flynn.

D'Esopo went through the door.

From his chair, Rutledge said, "Paul, wait for Flynn downstairs, will you?"

Wahler nodded and left, closing the door behind him.

Rutledge said: "Flynn, would it surprise you to know I've talked with the head of No Name this morning?"

"Yes."

"You're right. I haven't. And I wasn't about to say I had. You could find out I hadn't too easily."

"What you're trying to say is you believe you could, if you wanted to."

"Something like that. I have telephoned other people about you this morning. Since D'Esopo recommended you for this job last night."

" 'This job?' " asked Flynn. "I don't remember applying for a job."

"I know something of who you are, Flynn."

Discreetly, Flynn yawned. "You're trying to tell me you're more important than the Commissioner of Boston Police."

"I guess I am." Rutledge stood up. "I'm sure I don't need to present images to you of carrots and sticks." He shook hands with Flynn again, as if they had agreed on something. "Don't commit yourself in any way, Flynn, or talk to anyone, including your friend, Concannon, until you come back and talk to me."

"Kippered herrings," said Flynn.

"Beg pardon?"

"I wouldn't mind kippered herrings for breakfast. With my toast and marmalade."

5

"**T**he idea is, Flynn," Wahler said, turning the ignition key of the Rolls Royce, "you're staying in the motel, Timberbreak Lodge, down the road. It will be an easy matter for you to introduce yourself to the local police, and offer your assistance." He backed the car around. "They'll be delighted to have you confirm their findings."

In response, Flynn committed himself to silence.

The morning remained gray but the mist had lifted. Along the dirt road to the main gate of The Rod and Gun Club, the fog patches had left all but the deepest dells. The trees along the road seemed uniformly pine, tall and dark, with the odd stand of silver birch. On the rises of the road, broader views could be seen of October foliage muted by overcast.

The car was stopped at the gate. The armed guard came close enough to the car to ascertain there was no one in the back seat. He noted the names of the two men in the front seat on his clipboard.

As the car went through the gate, Flynn said, "He didn't check our pockets for the silverware."

"He has to know who is on the place and who has left, Flynn."

"Why?"

There was no answer.

On the paved road, they turned downhill.

"Are you Rutledge's driver?" Flynn asked. "Valet? Secretary?"

Wahler straightened one sleeve of his expensive three-piece suit. "Lawyer. I'm a graduate of Harvard Law School, member of the bar."

"Please accept my personal regrets," said Flynn.

"I'm not Rutledge's only lawyer, of course. Just the one closest to him. I sort of work things out with him, then translate his decisions to other lawyers and all the other people he has to deal with."

"So there is never any question about his expressing himself in a legal manner."

"That's right. Before he says or does anything, anything at all, all precedents and documents have been checked. By me."

"Ah, the modern world," said Flynn, spinning his Rs. "We're all just puppets dancing on strings pulled by lawyers."

"That's about right."

"Do you often travel with him?"

"Usually."

"What? Even on a weekend like this, huntin' and fishin'?"

Wahler did not answer right away. "Meetings go on at The Rod and Gun Club, Flynn." More easily, he said, "And there's always the telephone."

"Married yourself? Have a home life?"

Flynn guessed Wahler was in his early thirties.

"Not anymore. Was married. I have an apartment between Rutledge's home and his home office. His car picks me up most mornings, drops me off most nights."

"Home," Flynn hummed. "And as the young husband said to the gynecologist, 'What's in it for you?'"

"No one in the world has a better overview of his business than I have. I'm listed as an executor of his estate now." Gently, Wahler was braking the big car down a grade. "He controls many huge interests, Flynn. And I know them all as well or better than he does." Wahler crossed the yellow dividing line and turned off the road to the left into the parking lot of The Timberbreak Lodge. "Sooner or later, as gaps appear, I should be able to pick any position I want. Meantime, I walk around with his power in my pocket. And everyone knows it."

"And if Rutledge makes a mistake?" Flynn asked. "Is it the son of your mother named Paul who gets the blame?"

Wahler turned off the engine. "First we find the manager of the hotel. His name is Morris."

Only a few cars were in the motel driveway. One was dented, mud-splattered and said "Bellingham Police" in chipped paint on its side. Its appearance did not suggest much concern for image.

24

From down the road an old Cadillac hearse waddled into the parking lot. Two men in dark clothes with very white faces were on the front seat.

Standing beside the car, Flynn looked at Timberbreak Lodge. As a piece of architecture, it seemed oddly truncated. Its main office area, under a peaked roof, seemed almost the right size, but the one-store area for rooms extending from the reception area seemed uncommonly small. The lodge looked like a gaunt woman in a long dress.

Following Wahler into the reception area, Flynn hit his knuckles against the wall. He might as well have knocked against a match box. Cheap plywood, covered with a pine stain with no insulation or other building material behind it, he guessed.

The reception area was colder than outdoors.

"Morning, Mister Wahler," said the man behind the reception desk. He was a ruddy, outdoors type in a heavy woolen shirt.

"Morning," Wahler said. "This is Police Inspector Frank Flynn."

The man extended a heavily calloused hand over the counter.

"Pleased to meet you, Inspector. Sad business, this. Carl Morris, owner and manager of Timberbreak Lodge." He looked down at the reception book on the counter. "You're in Room 16, Inspector."

"Am I indeed? I'm liable to be anywhere."

"What room was Huttenbach's?" Wahler asked.

"Other side of the building. Room 22."

Across the reception lounge a huge window looked out over forested valley and hillsides. Flynn supposed the view would be dazzling, if the sun were out.

Open doorways led from the left and right of the lounge. Over one a wood-burned sign said "Rooms 11–16"; over the other, "Rooms 17–22."

"Is there a lower level to this place?" asked Flynn. "A downstairs?"

"Nope," Morris answered. "Just the one floor."

"Then you have only twelve guest rooms."

"We're a small lodge."

"You must have a pretty high room rate," Flynn shivered. "To pay the fuel bill. Not at all sure I can afford it."

Behind Morris was a closed door. Wood-burned on it were the words: "Manager Private." As they stood there, Flynn heard the voices of either two or three women talking, sometimes simultaneously.

"I see the Shaws are here." Morris had ducked his head to look through the front window. "Things have been moving slowly, I guess. Sunday morning. Chief Jensen is with the body now. I've told him you're here, Inspector. In a manner of speaking, of course." Morris allowed a small grin. "He's waiting for you. And Doc Allister is here." Morris' grin opened as he looked at Flynn. "Doc Allister gets something like a thousand a year from the county to play coroner. He's about the only doctor we got. At least, he's the oldest."

"Not a qualified pathologist," said Flynn.

"He's best at sending out bills." Morris came around the counter. "I'll bring you to them. You going to stay here, Mister Wahler?"

"Yes."

"We don't have a breakfast room, as you know. There's a Mister Coffee maker over there by the fireplace."

"Thanks." Hands in the pockets of his suit jacket, to warm himself, Wahler sat in a wicker chair in the lounge.

As Morris led Flynn through the main door and around the building he said, as if he could hardly wait for the opportunity, "It happened last night. About eleven. I was in the office just watching the late news. I heard the blast of a shotgun from outside the building. I rushed out and there was Huttenbach..."

There was Huttenbach.

They had gone a few meters onto unkempt grass from the path surrounding the lodge.

Face up on the grass lay the body of a young man. His head

26

and upper body were dotted with blood. One eye was still open. The other was half-closed, with a single dot of blood on the lid.

Two men stood nearby.

One said, "Inspector Wynn?"

"Flynn."

In gray mountain light of an October Sunday morn, two men shook hands over the corpse.

"Alfred Jensen. Bellingham Chief of Police. Well, I'm all the police there is in Bellingham. I'm also head of the town road department. Mostly, that means I'm in charge of snow removal. This here is Doc Allister. He's pretty much in charge of births and deaths 'round here, not much good in-between, if you're just sick."

Doc Allister had a big nose, which he lowered and raised in salute to Flynn.

"Death was instantaneous," Doctor Allister stated, showing he was not completely innocent of the formal language of the witness stand. "Result of a shotgun discharge. I would put the hour of death at somewhere around eleven o'clock last night."

"Where's the shotgun?" Flynn asked.

"In my car," Jensen said. "It's a pretty good one. Had his initials on it. *D. H.* It was lying right here when we found it."

Jensen pointed to the ground near Huttenbach's feet.

"Here's our funeral director," Jensen said. The two black-suited men from the hearse had come around the corner of the lodge. They walked in slow parade. "Shaw and son. Shaw's pa used to be the town drunk," Jensen said to Flynn. "Now Shaw is. Shaw's son is workin' on it. Depressing, undertaking. Hello, Fred!" Jensen said cheerily enough. "Glad you could make it."

Shaw's and son's blotchy faces nodded.

"We'll just let this Inspector inspect around a little, then you can take the body. Got your stretcher, or whatever you call it?"

Shaw looked at the rough ground.

"Better get somethin' to carry him off."

Flynn crouched by the body.

Indeed death had been instantaneous. There had been little bleeding. The young man's tweed jacket and light woolen shirt, opened at the throat, had been shredded by shotgun pellets. All his clothes, including his light corduroy trousers, socks and loafers, were rain-soaked as he lay. His hair was wet. A hank of hair matted on his forehead.

He was a slim, well-built young man, not more than thirty years old, if that. Flynn guessed his sports would have been squash racquets, handball, something that required speed, agility and brains rather than weight or brute force. His wrist watch was heavy gold. On his right wrist was a gold identification bracelet. A shotgun pellet had shattered one tooth. Other than that his teeth were white and even.

The grass around him had been washed by rain and stomped down by Carl Morris, Doctor Allister, Chief Jensen and whoever else.

Flynn lifted the late Congressman Huttenbach's left arm, felt it, and let it drop. Putting his death at about eleven the previous night was not far wrong, if wrong at all.

Knees snapping, Chief Jensen crouched beside Flynn. "Really appreciate your expert opinion on all this, Inspector. I know you big-city police guys see more of murders than you do of your own coffee cups."

"I don't use stimulants," Flynn said.

The nearest line of trees was more than two hundred meters down the hill from where they were crouching.

Chief Jensen was staring at the ground. "The man was killed by his own shotgun," he said slowly. "One barrel. We hear he has a wife and kids. Young man. Congressman from south of here, somewhere. It's easy enough to say he got killed accidentally while cleaning his shotgun." The Chief looked off at the line of trees. "That's what we say around here about most such suicides."

Flynn swiveled on the balls of his feet.

Shaw and son were pushing, pulling a metal framed stretcher on wheels over the rough ground toward them.

Flynn stood up. "No reason why you shouldn't move him. I take it you took photographs of all this."

"Yes, we did," Chief Jensen said happily. He stood up. "My son came out here at very first light and took pictures. He has one of those idiot-proof cameras, you know? And he'll turn them into the drugstore first thing in the morning. We should have 'em back Wednesday, Thursday."

"You took the photographs before you removed the shotgun?"

"Yes, we did," Jensen said proudly.

"Did you encase the shotgun so it can be examined for fingerprints?"

Jensen's face fell. "No. We didn't. What fingerprints could we expect on it? It was his own gun. His own initials were on the stock. It had already been rained on, last night, by the time we got here."

Flynn looked at Morris, standing nearby, smiling. His smile seemed to suggest he was ready to burst out singing, *Oh, what a beautiful morning.*

"If you're ready, Inspector, I'll show you the Congressman's room."

"Really appreciate all you're doing, Inspector," Chief Jensen crowed. "Us country boys don't get to see a real professional work too often. Damned nice of you to disturb your holiday weekend and come out and give us a hand. Busman's holiday, uh?"

Flynn stared at him.

"It will be fun to hear you give evidence, too," the Chief continued. "You'll give it right. As it should be done."

Flynn asked Morris, "Has Mrs. Huttenbach arrived yet?"

"Don't think so. Not by the time we came out here."

A gangly teenaged boy in a hunting cap came around the corner of the lodge and stopped. A camera hung on a strap from his neck. In his hand he had a notebook and ballpoint pen.

"There's the press, though," Chief Jensen said. He called, "Hi, Jimmy!"

Doctor Allister was already walking toward the Voice of the People.

Jensen hurried over to him, too. "Thought you were at your grandmother's this weekend, Jimmy. Ain't she eighty?"

"I came back," the boy said. "Patty called me and said there'd been a mor-der."

29

Doctor Allister's beak bobbed as he dictated into the notebook what he had to say to the world.

"Show me the room you gave Huttenbach," Flynn said to Morris. "Even the White Queen can believe six things before breakfast."

Silently, Wahler drove Flynn back up the paved road, along the dirt road, and through the check point in the tall, miles-long fence surrounding The Rod and Gun Club.

Just as they were cresting the last hill before coming to the lake, a helicopter roared up from behind the clubhouse. When it got well above tree level, it turned, and still gaining altitude, flew southeast.

"My, my," said Flynn. "It seems not everybody gets in and out through the hole in the fence. Some fly away under blades of steel."

6

"**G**rover," Flynn found himself grumbling into the telephone. To the switchboard of The Old Records Building on Craigie Street, Flynn properly had asked for Sergeant Richard T. Whelan, but once hearing the voice of the man himself answer he could not restrain himself from addressing him by the nickname Flynn had given him but Sergeant Whelan never had accepted.

And Grover did not restrain himself from a prolonged sigh. "Yes, Inspector? Not coming in today?"

It was well past ten o'clock Sunday morning. Flynn seldom went to the office Sundays, which was why Grover usually did.

Taylor had met Wahler and Flynn at the door. The guard had phoned ahead their arrival. Taylor said he had put Flynn's breakfast in his room.

Taylor led the way upstairs, to show Flynn his room. But Flynn went to the wide doorway of the club's grand hall and looked in.

A skinny old man, totally naked, sat in a chair by the fire, reading. In the changing firelight the white skin and heavy blue veins of his legs and feet had almost the effect of a flashing neon light.

Behind Flynn, Wahler said under his breath, "That's Wendell Oland. He doesn't like to wear clothes."

"And who is he when he's dressed?"

"Senior partner at a major law firm. Income in the millions a year."

Still dressed for fishing, shoeless, Senator Dunn Roberts sat in a chair within reach of the bar table. Even from across the big room, Flynn could see the man was despondently drunk. He might as well have been sitting in a slum doorway.

"Looks like the Senator missed breakfast," commented Flynn.

"Not much."

Four men, one in a heavy, torn bathrobe, sat at a poker

table down the room, playing seriously, silently. The only currency visible, blue in the firelight, was in one hundred dollar demoninations.

"A quiet Sunday morning in the country," said Flynn.

In Flynn's room instead of tea or coffee a silver pot of plain hot water for his herbal tea had been laid out, as well as a half grapefruit and French toast.

"Thoughtful of you," Flynn said to Taylor. "Been working here long?"

Flynn lowered his tea bag into the pot of hot water.

"Just since last spring."

"Are you from around here?"

"I'm from New York City."

"Rather dead around here, isn't it?"

Taylor's ready grin filled his face again. "Getting deader every minute."

Flynn saw that Cocky had been in. The chess set was laid out on a side table.

White pawn had been moved to King Four.

Flynn moved Black Pawn to King Four.

"Anything else you want, sir?"

"Just need to make a couple of phone calls after breakfast."

"Right, sir. Dial seven, wait till you hear a clear line, then dial your number."

So Flynn made the most of his breakfast and called Grover.

"I was called away," Flynn said lamely.

"On another one of your mysterious trips, Frank?"

Grover doubtlessly had his own explanation, or explanations, for Flynn's odd disappearances. Flynn had no idea what such explanations might be, but he was sure they lacked both accuracy and imagination. Not being able to explain his absences himself, he had never been able to enquire how Grover saw them.

"I'm on a trip, yes," Flynn admitted. "And, yes, it is mysterious."

"I bet."

"Lieutenant Concannon is with me."

A snort assaulted Flynn's ear. "Hadn't noticed him missing."

32

"Grover, I'm particularly interested in that hit-and-run bicycle death on Tremont Street last night."

"No one else is."

"You mean, you aren't. What have you done so far?"

"This old man was knocked off his bicycle and run over by a car traveling south at high speed about eight fifteen last night. Dead on arrival. A female witness said she could not give a description of car or driver, she was too horrified, she said, but she was able to say the car didn't stop."

"Didn't stop at all? Not even slow down?"

"Didn't even slow down. Just went through the intersection at high speed."

"I doubt you could hit an old man on a bicycle, run over and kill him and not know something had happened. How many people were in the car?" Flynn asked.

Again Grover seemed to be referring to the scene-of-the-accident report. "Just the driver. She was pretty sure of that. 'One head in the car,' she said."

"Male?"

"She thinks so, but not sure. It was dark out."

"A peculiar time of day for it, Grover. A peculiar time of day."

"What's so peculiar?"

"Don't most hit-and-run accidents happen just after the bars close for the night? And how many old men do you see pedaling a bicycle through city streets after dark?"

"Inspector, here you go again. Two damned fools bump into each other, one of 'em gets dead, and you want to turn the police department inside out."

For a brief moment, Flynn envisioned turning Grover inside out. Revealed might be the perfect vacuum.

"You mean, Grover," he said softly, slowly, "you suspect the bicyclist of contributory negligence?"

Usually, Flynn was uncertain of using such terms, as he really did not know what they meant. He never hesitated using such terms with Grover, however, as he knew Grover was less certain of their meaning than he was.

"You trying to solve your case load by telephone now, Inspector?"

33

"I might forwarder," Flynn grumbled, "with able assistance."

"I'm on the Police Eats Committee, Inspector. We're having a big lunch meeting at the Hotex Lenox."

"Grover, I think you know how enthusiastic I am about the level of the culinary arts in the police commissaries being raised above the standard taco."

"You don't like tacos?"

"Have you yet compiled a list of all cars reported stolen last night after eight fifteen?"

"What? No."

"Isn't that the thing to do?" asked Flynn. "Don't people who hit-and-run almost invariably report their cars stolen within an hour or two of the incident? Surely, I would."

"Inspector, I'm not going to have time. Each one of us has to count the snack and candy dispensers —"

"Fortified by the nice lunch at the Hotel Lenox, Grover, you may not have as much time, but surely you'll have more energy."

"Inspector, if you think this is so damned important, why don't you come back —"

"I'll call you later, Grover, in hopes of your having found a car reported stolen with bits of old man and bicycle still adhered to it."

Flynn then called Elsbeth and read off the number of his telephone to her.

Cocky entered the room just as Flynn had poured out the last cup of lukewarm tea in the pot and lit his pipe.

"Did they feed you, Cocky? Are you the one who got the kippered herrings?"

"French toast," said Cocky, going to the chessboard. "Dwight Huttenbach. Age twenty-nine. Married once, Carol Kroepsch, daughter of an upper New York State lawyer with real estate, banking and political interests. Two children: a son,

Dwight, they call 'Ike'; a daughter, Mary. The Huttenbachs, as you probably know, are an old line family of great wealth. One of Huttenbach's uncles is an ambassador. Huttenbach himself took a liberal arts degree from the University of Virginia, majoring in government, minoring in economics. This is his first term in Congress. The only piece of major legislation he's introduced so far had to do with pollution."

"You'd think a lad like that would go on to law school."

"Academic record apparently not good enough for a first-class law school. He played tennis for the University of Virginia, is an A-ranked handball player. He also played trumpet."

"Musical, was he? Classical trumpet, jazz?"

"He liked to play trumpet in marching bands. Would show up at political rallies with his trumpet, and join the band. On Fourth of July he'd go from town to town in his district and play the trumpet in the parades."

"What a splendid device," mused Flynn, "for a young politician with nothing to say."

From Cocky's silence, Flynn gathered he had concluded his report. "What a marvel you are, Cocky. How did you find out all that?"

Cocky shrugged his right shoulder. "Called Daphne at Old Records. She works Sundays."

"Well. . ." Flynn inhaled on his pipe and let the smoke out slowly as he talked. "Would you believe a twenty-nine year old Congressman, away for a hunting weekend, would have unpacked his suitcase completely, hung every trouser and jacket neatly in a motel room closet, organized every shirt, undergarment and sock in appropriate drawers of the dresser, removed the blade from his razor without replacing it, screwed the cap on his toothpaste, left a bottle of good Scotch whiskey unopened on his bureau and have *The Federalist,* without a bookmark, mind you, on his nightstand?"

Over the chessboard, Cocky turned his face to Flynn, so Flynn could see him smile.

Flynn said, "So far, the set is worth the price of admission."

Cocky said, "I can't find the telephone switchboard."

Flynn glanced at the phone by his bed.

35

"You'd think a big place like this, all these important people here, would need a telephone switchboard."

"Indeed I would," agreed Flynn. "By the way, Cocky, who was that who took off in the helicopter?"

"Walter March."

"Suppose he just went out to buy a newspaper?" Flynn put on his jacket. "I think Rutledge was expecting me an hour or two ago. I trust this time he has something to say, and the goodness to say it." Watching Cocky over the chessmen, Flynn asked, "Stumped already?"

Cocky moved Pawn to King Bishop Four.

Flynn took Cocky's Pawn.

Cocky moved his Knight to King Bishop Three.

"Ach." Flynn put his pipe in his jacket pocket. "You want me to think, do you?"

"I think, Inspector, this will be one of our more unusual games."

7

Paul Wahler, still dressed for Wall Street, opened the door to Suite 23 at Flynn's knock.

Inside the living room of the suite, Charles Rutledge turned, saw Flynn, and immediately hung up the phone.

"Well, Flynn." Rutledge now was dressed in a loose tweed jacket and gray flannel slacks. He glanced at his watch. "Almost lunch time."

"That's all right with me," said Flynn. "My breakfast came disguised as French toast."

"Doubt you'll do much better for lunch. You know these private clubs."

"Do I?"

"I mean, it's hard to keep cooks. It's hard to get cooks who are much good in the first place to come up here and live in the woods. Cooks are like moths: attracted to heat and bright lights."

Rutledge smiled his appreciation at his own simile to Wahler, who smiled his appreciation back.

"Well, Flynn, did you inspect the scene of the accident?"

"Accident..." mused Flynn. "I surveyed the scene of a grand mistake."

Rutledge glanced at the open door, nodded to Wahler. Wahler closed the door to the corridor.

"Sit down, Flynn, and tell me what you mean."

Again Rutledge sat with his back to the window light. Flynn sat in a flowered two-seat divan.

Wahler opened a folder on his lap and occasionally made a note in it.

"It's a critic you want," said Flynn. "One with a special interest in stage sets. A stage set, you know, is designed so action taking place in it is made credible."

Wahler took a note.

Rutledge waited for Flynn to go on.

"Even if your boy-Congressman were suffering from

37

Angelism, any fool could tell you he did not unpack himself in that motel room, or spend a minute in it. I can tell a professional unpacking job when I see it. Your butler named Taylor, was it? He unpacked me in the same precise manner while I was down admiring his handiwork at Timberbreak Lodge."

"Huttenbach's things were placed in a reasonable manner in the room at Timberbreak Lodge," Wahler stated.

"If the local police aren't prone to notice," Flynn said, "his wife will, when she comes to pack him up."

"His wife is here," Rutledge said. "She is distraught, of course. A friend drove her up. Carl Morris showed her the room, briefly. Morris is packing Huttenbach's things."

"Um . . ." Flynn ran his hand over his jaw and remembered the early hour at which he had shaved. "Even a great director can't make a bad stage set work."

"The scene of the accident, Flynn," Rutledge said.

"What accident?" Flynn looked summarily at Rutledge. "He was murdered."

"Yes, yes," said Rutledge. "But how do you know?"

"How could anyone not know? A young man took his shotgun outside, at eleven o'clock at night, to a lightless place, to clean it? I don't know what time it began to rain here last night, but my guess is that eleven o'clock the temperature was no more than ten degrees centigrade. This young man went outdoors at that hour in that weather to clean his shotgun dressed in a tweed jacket, light woolen shirt, open collar? Or perhaps you're going to tell me he was heading out at that hour, dressed that way, on an expedition to shoot snipe . . ."

"His behavior isn't inconsistent with someone committing suicide," Wahler stated.

"No behavior is inconsistent with someone committing suicide." Then Flynn smiled broadly. "But why would a young man commit suicide with *The Federalist* waiting for him on his bedside table?"

Wahler smiled wanly and took a note.

Flynn sighed. "A shotgun pellet went through his upper lip and shattered one tooth. Another entered his eye and did its killing work. Good God, man." Flynn sighed again. "A man

38

aiming a shotgun at himself and pulling the trigger would blow his head completely off, unless he had arms the lengths of telephone poles. Have you no idea how it would look? Your man, Dwight Huttenbach, was shot from a considerable distance away, surely from outside his own reach!"

Astutely, Wahler said, "We should have blasted him from close-up."

"And you can't tell me you're fooling for a minute these country boys you've assembled as discoverers of the evidence! A country doctor, a country sheriff, a country mortician. They're insulting you by going along with this charade!"

Rutledge shifted his feet on the rug.

"I'm sure it's hard scrubbing a living out of these hills," Flynn continued. "And I'm also sure the good citizens 'round here have every reason to consider the welfare of their own families 'way ahead of the question as to how some rich kid from far away happened to have his brain penetrated by shotgun pellets. But I trust whatever it is you're paying them, it's in the true coin of the realm, not just the currency of fear and intimidation."

Rutledge was looking calmly at Wahler. "So what's your conclusion, Flynn?"

"I feel like a schoolchild," said Flynn, "having to recite my multiplication tables before going home. Huttenbach did not shoot himself. From the state of the bottoms of his shoes, I would say he was shot indoors, most likely in a fairly large room. He was shot here, at The Rod and Gun Club. It wouldn't take me many minutes to find that room. He wasn't shot in the grand hall downstairs; I've already looked — unless you have closets full of replacement lampshades, rugs and window glass. After he was dead, his belongings were moved into Room 22 at Timberbreak Lodge. And his body was laid out next to Timberbreak Lodge with very little attention paid to appearances. Good grief," Flynn said. "His hair was even matted on his forehead. Not a very likely occurrence for someone shot from the front and blown backwards!"

Rutledge continued his calm gaze at Wahler.

Wahler said, "As Inspector Flynn pointed out, it was dark out there."

In his soft voice, Flynn expostulated, "Of all the arrogance!"

"Flynn," Rutledge said, "we're trying to spare his family."

"Is that the truth?" snapped Flynn. "We've already established it wasn't suicide."

"There's a certain onus even to murder—"

"Bloody well right," said Flynn. "People die of it! I'll tell you what the onus is." Flynn sat forward. "Huttenbach was staying here, at The Rod and Gun Club. Huttenbach was murdered here, at The Rod and Gun Club. And you boys truly don't know who murdered him, or why. But you care less about that than you do about something else. So in the dead of night, Wahler and Taylor and I don't yet know who else, move his body off the property, outside the fence, down to Timberbreak Lodge. And you move his belongings into Timberbreak Lodge and scatter them about with the precision of a computer. And you get Carl Morris, for a decent amount of change, I expect, to agree that Huttenbach was staying at Timberbreak Lodge for the weekend. And that he was killed there. Then you arrange to have me come up, pretend I'm registered at Timberbreak Lodge itself, to give some big-city authority to the paid-for findings of the Chief of Bellingham's Road Department. And in what coin of what realm do you expect to pay me?" Flynn sat back in his chair. "All you're concerned about is keeping The Rod and Gun Club out of it."

Rutledge stood up and went into his bedroom. He returned with a shotgun.

From a bookcase, he took two rags and a can of gun oil.

"You're every bit the man I thought you were, Flynn."

Rutledge sat down, broke open the gun, and checked to see the barrels were empty. Then he began cleaning it.

Rutledge laughed. "Don't know what we would have done, if you'd come back from Timberbreak Lodge having believed— or saying you believed—all our arranged evidence. Then we would have had a problem." He ran an index finger along the oiled barrel, apparently just for the pleasure of it. "Wahler will take you downstairs in a few minutes to show you where Huttenbach was murdered."

"In the middle of the night," Wahler stated, "it isn't easy to arrange anything that would even fit into the category of a hunting accident."

"You'd be surprised, Flynn"—Rutledge squinted down one barrel, then another—"if you knew some of the names who approved of our midnight decision, however faulty it appears to you."

"Faulty and criminal," said Flynn.

"Criminal," Rutledge said easily. "Yes."

"Governor Caxton Wheeler," Flynn said, "was departing as we were arriving. At dawn."

"God!" Wahler grinned. "His valet-bodyguard-driver! It's impossible to get him to move! They call him Flash because he's so incredibly slow!"

"Is he someone else who helped move the body?" Flynn asked.

Waher said, "Yes."

"Walter March took off in a helicopter a couple of hours ago."

"Yes, he did," said Rutledge. "Our members have to keep to their own schedules."

"And," said Flynn, "I don't know what the hell I'm doing sitting here, letting you clean that shotgun before my very eyes!"

"You're being understanding, Flynn," said Rutledge evenly.

"Understanding, am I? A less phlegmatic man might be having apoplexy! You know I have no power in this jurisdiction to make arrests!"

Wahler said, "We know."

"Huttenbach's father was an old friend," said Rutledge. "From schooldays. His father was a founder of The Rod and Gun Club. I knew him, too."

"And when young Huttenbach wanted to run for Congress . . . ?"

"Some of us here at The Rod and Gun Club have been advising him all along. Actually, since before he started school."

"Grooming him, you mean," said Flynn.

"Advising him to make the most of his opportunities,"

41

amended Rutledge. "Dwight had a brilliant future." Rutledge
tested the pull on the shotgun's triggers. "It may not seem it to
you at the moment, Flynn, moving his body in the middle of the
night and so on, building a stage set, as you call it, but we're
deeply concerned about Dwight's murder." Rutledge snapped
the shotgun closed. "We want it investigated. We want to know
who did this and why."

Rutledge leaned the shotgun against his chair.

Flynn rubbed his forehead. "You want me to run a private
investigation."

Rutledge said, "You got it."

"And how can I investigate when there can be no control
over the situation? When all the evidence has been tampered
with before I got here? When a potential presidential candidate
slips through the hole in the fence at dawn? When a major
American newspaper publisher helicopters out of here between
breakfast and lunch?"

"Ah," said Rutledge. "Now you see one of the problems.
You may not be pleased at our use of local authorities, term us
'arrogant', as you did, but do you think the Inspector of Roads
could get control over this situation?"

"State authorities could get control," said Flynn, "if you
gave it to them."

"Have Caxton's name dragged through a murder
investigation? Have Walter's competing newspapers hint at his
complicity in a shotgun killing?"

"Have it revealed unto the world," countered Flynn, "that
such a place as The Rod and Gun Club exists?"

Rutledge stood, wandered behind his chair, and looked
through the small window.

"That's the fact of life, Flynn. That's what you're dealing
with. Local police aren't equipped to investigate this incident,
and you know it. And we do want it investigated quickly and
well. D'Esopo named you, and you are the man for the job."

"You've got to understand," Wahler offered humbly, "the
members of The Club, well, when they have a legal problem,
they call in the top attorney in the country for advice. When
they have a medical problem —"

42

"I'm complimented," said Flynn. "When they need bread, they have toast."

"They've gotten in a special private investigator," Wahler concluded lamely.

"What you've run into here, Flynn," said Rutledge looking through the window at thousands of fenced-in acres, "is privacy. An idea diminished by contemporary society, but still, not a bad idea at all."

"And what other problems do I have?" asked Flynn.

"Another problem is pretty obvious," Rutledge said to the window pane. "Obviously, the bastard who shot Dwight Huttenbach is one of us."

"Ach, tell me something I didn't know," said Flynn. "And when I catch the bastard, what do you want me to do with him — privately?"

Rutledge turned and looked down at his feet. "We'll see." He cleared his throat. "I can assure you, Flynn, no one here is going to go off half-cocked. We have our own resources. Considerable resources. At The Rod and Gun Club the members consult with each other constantly. There will be no decisions independently made."

Flynn thought of a recent bank robbery in Boston. One of the desperately nervous robbers shot another robber when the second robber didn't obey fast enough. The first robber, besides being indicted for bank robbery, was also charged with attempted murder while committing a felony.

Wahler said, "I'll bring you down and show you where Huttenbach was killed."

"And I can assure you, Rutledge," Flynn said, standing up, "that when it comes time for your special investigator, and my portable witness, Concannon, to testify, you'll hear nothing from our mouths but the truth, the whole truth, and nothing but the truth."

"We'll see." Rutledge turned his back on Flynn, again to look through the small window. "If this matter is disposed of correctly, there might never be reason for anyone to testify."

8

"**T**here are two people at table I expect you don't know," Charles Rutledge said at the beginning of lunch. He smiled engagingly at the man seated at the thick round table. "At least I hope you have no reason to know. I think most of you have met Boston Police Commissioner D'Esopo."

Eddy D'Esopo sat across the round table from Rutledge in his double-knit jacket, his heavy face lined with sleeplessness.

"D'Esopo is not a member, as you know, but has been a guest two or three times the last year." From where he was seated, Rutledge turned his open face to the right, to Flynn. "This, gentlemen, is Inspector Francis Xavier Flynn, a man whose background does not invite delving into. Suffice it to say, he has a brilliant record of running discreet investigations, let's say, above the salt, with spectacular results."

"Shall I dance around the ring?" gently inquired Flynn, putting on what he hoped would be seen as a wry smile.

Rutledge turned his face to Cocky seated across from Flynn, looking small and misshapen among the big, ruddy, well-cared-for men. "And this is Detective Lieutenant Walter Concannon who, I understand, took early retirement from the Boston Police some while ago. We weren't really expecting Concannon, but under the circumstances, a guest of Flynn's necessarily is a guest of ours."

Cocky kept his eyes in his empty stew bowl.

At a table near the kitchen door Taylor stood with another white-coated man, Vietnamese, awaiting the courtesies to be over.

Around the big dining room panelled in barnwood there were several other round tables, smaller, not set for lunch. Large leaded windows on one wall overlooked the lake.

"Never thought we'd be entertaining investigators of any kind at The Rod and Gun Club," Rutledge said, "but you all know of the tragic occurrence of last night, and those preliminary steps we have taken so far."

44

"Threw it all down the hill." Naked, seventy year old Wendell Oland sat at table to Flynn's left. Formerly, Flynn had dined with naked people, of course, but he could not remember having done so formally. "Quite right, too."

Rutledge said, "I promised Flynn he will have the cooperation of each and every one of us. It was agreed last night, gentlemen, that *we* want to know what happened and why before *we* decide what to do about it."

At first Flynn welcomed the flurry of skirt, the flash of stockinged leg, the tumble of silken hair which then appeared in the small door of the dining room.

Then he realized how ungainly the apparition was.

The person wearing these clothes was tall, broad-shouldered, and needed a shave.

"Ah, Lauderdale," chided Rutledge. "Late again."

"That's Judge Lauderdale," Wahler whispered from Flynn's right. "He likes to wear dresses."

"He doesn't wear them well," observed Flynn.

The man's wig was off several degrees counterclockwise, his blouse screwed several degrees off clockwise, and the skirt was twisted counterclockwise. His stockings sagged.

"He keeps closets of 'em here," Wahler whispered.

"Can't say I don't hear the damned gong," Lauderdale said. "It gives me migraine." The Judge pronounced it *me-graine.* "It rushes me so."

Lauderdale sat between Wahler and D'Esopo.

From below his shaggy eyebrows, Eddy D'Esopo was looking worriedly at Flynn. He then looked worriedly at Cocky.

"Permit me to finish the introductions." Rutledge began at his immediate left. "Clifford...Arlington..." He skipped Cocky. "...Buckingham...Ashley..." He skipped D'Esopo. "...Lauderdale..." He skipped Wahler and Flynn. "...Oland..." Rutledge looked at the empty place set immediately to his right. "I guess Dunn Roberts didn't make it to lunch. Must be out hunting."

"He's napping," Lauderdale said.

"Crocked," said Ashley. "Drank his breakfast. He'll feel the better for it."

45

Clifford, Arlington, Buckingham and Ashley were those who had been playing poker so earnestly upon Flynn's return to the clubhouse. Ashley had since changed from a bathrobe to a hunting jacket.

Rutledge nodded toward the kitchen door.

Taylor and the waiter began going around the table ladling stew into the bowls.

"What about the gong?" Flynn quietly asked Wahler.

The Sunday noon peace of the hills had been devastated by the sound of the gong, struck once. At its sound, Wahler had led Flynn from the storage room to the dining room.

"Everything around here happens to the sound of the gong. Breakfast, lunch, sauna, swim, dinner. It's a tradition."

"But where is it?" asked Flynn.

"Outside, on the kitchen porch."

"It must be pretty big."

"Damned big," agreed Wahler. "Damned big noise."

It took Flynn a moment to realize the naked man to his left was addressing him. "I never had much to do with criminal law."

"I can tell," said Flynn.

The naked man carefully placed his napkin on his right thigh. Stew was being ladled into his bowl.

"Have you investigated the scene of the crime?"

"Both," answered Flynn. "Considerate of your membership to give me a choice."

Wendell Oland looked regretfully at Flynn as stew was ladled into Flynn's bowl.

"I'd like to know," Wendell Oland said, sticking the spoon into his stew, "what bastard shot holes in my new waterproofs."

Buckingham filled his glass from the keg of beer on its own stand near the kitchen door.

Ashley asked, "What have you detected so far, Flynn?"

Each member at the table had taken a hard roll from a basket handed around.

Next to him, Oland had broken open his roll and was making small bread pellets out of it.

"Dwight Huttenbach was murdered last night at about eleven o'clock in what you call the storage room at The Rod and

46

Gun Club. He was standing near the north side of the room when he was shot. The murderer was standing at the south side of the room, near the door to the back corridor of the clubhouse. Possibly, if the door were open, he stood behind the door. In any case, it's a conjecture at this point that Huttenbach may have opened the door, entered, not closed the door, and not seen his murderer until he walked to the north side of the long room and then turned around. The weapon was a shotgun. Besides putting holes in Mister Oland's new waterproofs, the blast also blew out two small, high windows, wrecked several cross-country skis, ski parkas and other coats hanging on the far wall."

"We don't use 'Mister' at The Rod and Gun Club, Flynn," reminded Rutledge.

"If I were willing to be a member," answered Flynn, "I'd be willing to obey your rules."

D'Esopo looked sharply at Flynn. He got up and got himself a beer from the keg.

"What shotgun killed him?" asked Arlington.

"There are several shotguns stored in that room," answered Flynn. "Fifteen, to be exact."

"Mostly we keep them for guests," said Ashley, trying his stew.

Buckingham, too, was making his roll into bread balls.

"Ballistics tests on shotguns aren't much good," said Flynn. "Plus, in that storeroom, there are cases of ammunition of various kinds, hunting rifles, various kinds of fishing gear, skis, ice skates, and, one music box."

"You found my music box?" exclaimed Lauderdale.

"It plays *The Wedding March,*" said Flynn. "From the Second Act of Wagner's *Lohengrin. F* is missing."

"My music box!" Lauderdale clasped his hands in front of his flat chest. "He found my music box! What a detective!"

Beside Lauderdale's plate was a smashed roll and an assortment of bread balls.

"Then," said Flynn, "most evidence was criminally destroyed, or altered. The corpse was moved ten or twelve kilometers, and placed outside Timberbreak Lodge. Generally, the scene of the crime was so disturbed there is little reason for

47

examining it much further. The victim's personal belongings, as much as I know of them, were also removed to the lodge. Outside the lodge an ersatz scene of crime was carelessly arranged. It is a useless source of evidence. The motel operators, I suspect the local police authority, others, the county coroner, apparently have been bribed into a willingness to give false evidence, to perjure themselves." After tasting it, Flynn considered his stew a moment. He wondered how anyone could make venison stew so bland. "Quite a catalog of crimes, gentlemen, for such a few short hours."

"Oh, my," said Lauderdale. "I just knew I shouldn't have come this weekend. And my son was so hoping I'd get to his football game. But I just had to get away."

"Why doesn't everyone at table state right here and now where he was last night at eleven o'clock?" said Clifford.

"There speaks the man with the perfect alibi," said Flynn.

"There speaks a man who reads mystery novels," said Ashley.

"Actually, not," said Clifford. "Wrong in both cases."

"You don't read mysteries?" said Ashley. "You never read *Don Quixote*?"

"I went to my room about nine thirty. I was asleep by quarter to ten."

Clifford was the youngest at the table. Flynn guessed he was in his early twenties. His dark blue sweat shirt complemented his wide, dark eyes and neatly clipped black hair. The skin over his prominent cheekbones was tight and clear and slightly touched by sun even in October. His neck was muscular and suggested an athletic body. Of everyone at the table, he had appeared to be listening most intently to Flynn.

"So was I, so was I," said Buckingham. "In my room early, asleep. I didn't even hear the shot."

"You were passed out," said Lauderdale.

"Yes," said Buckingham. "I'd had a lot to drink. Long before ten o'clock."

"Long before six o'clock," said Lauderdale.

"We don't watch that sort of thing around here," said Rutledge. "We surely don't comment on it."

In his fifties, Buckingham had the large, wide-open face

that almost seems to be a guarantee of success in business or politics. Such a face, rightly or wrongly, gives the impression of a bigness and frankness on the part of the man himself. Flynn had the sense of having seen photographs of Buckingham. At least Buckingham's hair was thinner than agreed with some previous knowledge of Buckingham's face. He had the build of someone who had played college football a generation before. And if he'd had too much to drink the night before, Flynn thought, studying him, he was not showing much sign of it at lunch the next day.

"What time did we finish playing gin?" Ashley leaned against the table and asked Arlington.

"About ten fifteen, ten thirty. Then I went into the television room to look at my local news off the Betamax."

Arlington, too, looked vaguely familiar. The curious thing about him was that his body was short and flabby; his face not at all fat or sagged. His eyebrows rose unnaturally at their outer ends, giving him a peculiarly supercilious expression. Flynn suspected that close examination would reveal scars of cosmetic surgery along his hairline, above and below his ears, under his jaw. Arlington looked in his early fifties but Flynn guessed he was in his mid-sixties.

"And I went for a walk," said Ashley. "I walked around the lake."

"That takes just an hour," Rutledge told Flynn.

"In the dark?" asked Flynn.

"There's a path."

"When I came back the shooting had taken place. Perhaps I heard it. I'm not sure. Apt to get sort of abstracted, when I walk."

Ashley was no more overweight than a normally healthy man is, in his mid-forties. His complexion was ruddy enough, but partly the source of his ruddiness was broken veins, and his eyes were liverish. Of all the men there, Ashley seemed to have given himself the closest shave, the most careful combing job.

"You were counting the days," Lauderdale said, "until you have to declare yourself a bankrupt."

Ashley glanced at Lauderdale. As he reached for his roll, Ashley's hand shook.

"When I came back," Ashley said, "I found everyone in the storage room. Poor Huttenbach lying there, bits of him on the wall."

"Ashley's not going bankrupt," Buckingham said loudly. "When did The Rod and Gun Club ever let one of its members go bankrupt?"

Lauderdale said: "When it serves our purposes."

In his early fifties, Lauderdale's extreme thinness could not diminish his bones, his man's shoulders beneath his blouse, the big knuckles of his hands. Clearly, Judge Lauderdale would look far more graceful in his judicial gown.

Flynn asked Ashley, "Precisely who was in the storage room when you arrived?"

"Everyone. Not Buckingham." Ashley looked around the table. "Everyone but Buckingham."

"Was Taylor there?"

Taylor and the waiter had retreated to the kitchen.

Several nodded affirmation.

"How was Taylor dressed?" asked Flynn.

"In shorts," Lauderdale said definitely.

"Shorts? You mean, undershorts?"

"No, just shorts. Those flimsy, short, running-short things. Barefooted. Shirtless. Sweating."

Clifford looked evenly at Flynn. "Just shorts."

"Where were you, Judge Lauderdale?" Flynn enjoyed asking.

"Actually, I was in my tub. Soaking. I had a face cloth folded over my eyes, as I lay back, soaking. There was the bang of the gun. The face cloth plopped into the water in front of me, I was so startled. It was all I could do to get on my chemise and mules and run down to see what happened."

"Soaking wet," said the naked Oland. "You did well not to catch cold."

"I may have a sniffle," Lauderdale sniffed.

Wahler leaned over and whispered to Flynn: "You realize all this is an act. Away from here Lauderdale is as straight as a Texas road. He just puts this on to entertain the boys."

"Is that why he does it?" asked Flynn.

"I was reading by the fire," Oland offered. "I may have

fallen asleep. The shot awoke me. I had gone to considerable trouble to get my new waterproofs. I was alone in the main room at the time."

Oland, well into his seventies, seemed the most relaxed of all sitting at the table. A skinny old man with thinning hair, tired eyes, a small pot low on his stomach, he seemed perfectly comfortable being the only naked person in the room.

"Do you remember what time Ashley and Arlington left the main room?" Flynn asked.

Oland thought a moment. "I don't remember them being there at all. I doubt they were."

Flynn asked Ashley and Arlington, "You were playing cards in the main room, weren't you?"

Both men said, "Yes."

"I doubt they were," repeated Oland. ·

"That leaves Wahler and me, I guess," said Rutledge. "We were together in my suite until about quarter to eleven. I had taken a shower, gotten into bed, and read a few pages when I heard the shot. It was seven minutes past eleven by my watch."

Everyone looked at Wahler.

"I came down to the main room, mixed myself a Scotch and soda, and took it out onto the front veranda."

"You went out without a coat?"

"I was wearing my suit jacket and vest. I didn't intend to leave the porch. I wanted some fresh air."

"And Senator Roberts?" Flynn asked the room.

"I don't know." Rutledge looked at others at the table. "Anyone know where Roberts was?"

No one seemed to know where Roberts was.

"How was he dressed when he arrived in the storage room?"

"In bathrobe and slippers," said Lauderdale.

"Yes," said Clifford. "I think so. He was carrying a book."

"And where were you?" Flynn asked Boston Police Commissioner Eddy D'Esopo.

"When I heard the shot?" the Commissioner asked absently.

"I think you've been hearing the conversation," Flynn said softly.

51

D'Esopo smiled foolishly. Then he laughed. "I was trying to commit burglary. Breaking and entering. I was in the kitchen, trying to find something to eat. The refrigerators were locked. All the cupboards were locked."

Laughter rose from the table.

"Of course they were locked," said Arlington. "What's so unusual about that?"

Testily, Oland said, "Such things are always locked at that hour."

Embarrassed, D'Esopo said, "I didn't know it."

"You learn that at school, man," said Buckingham.

"A good thing, too," said Oland. "Can't have people running in and out of the kitchen grabbing things at all hours. Makes things impossible for the servants."

Clifford was giving D'Esopo a friendly smile, which D'Esopo was feeling too miserable to accept.

Clifford had rolled an immense number of bread pellets beside his plate.

"And what about Governor Wheeler and Walter March?" Flynn asked Rutledge.

"I know earlier they were in the study, talking privately. They were in the storage room when I arrived. I presumed they had come from the study."

"Was anyone else here last night?" Flynn asked mildly. "Anyone else who exited through the fence at dawn, or flew away up the chimney?"

"No," said Rutledge. "Members come and go at The Rod and Gun Club as we please, Flynn. No one else was here last night. That is to say, only Wheeler and March have left. They had legitimate business elsewhere. And we've talked about that, telephonically, since you raised the issue. It's been agreed that both gentlemen will be available to you by phone, to answer any questions you may have, at any time. If you feel it's necessary to interview them personally, transportation will be provided."

"Cooperative of you," commented Flynn. "And do any of you gentlemen have any immediate plans to have legitimate business elsewhere?"

"Ashley will stay here," Lauderdale said. "Until his problems are solved."

"Want to see how this thing comes out," Oland said. "Who shot my waterproofs."

Around the table, no one else admitted plans to go, or openly agreed to stay.

"So," Flynn finally said, smiling across the table at Cocky, "each of you gentlemen here, in fact, states you were alone last night at seven minutes past eleven."

"That's not unusual," Rutledge said. "Such an hour is usually regarded as being after bedtime."

"And you're all here without wives, or girl friends, people with whom you might share your beds."

Rutledge shrugged. "That's tradition."

"The charmin' thing is," said Flynn, "none of you is providing an alibi for anyone else."

Clifford was brushing all his bread balls into his left hand.

"We all hope for a speedy resolution of this affair," said Rutledge. "We are cooperating as much as we can."

Using an open, overhanded throw, Clifford threw a bread ball at Oland. It hit him in the face.

Then Clifford fired another at D'Esopo.

D'Esopo sat back, totally startled.

Oland threw a bread ball at Rutledge.

Beside Flynn, Wahler leaned over.

Bread balls were flying through the air, in all directions.

Lauderdale stood up to accomplish a wide, full-armed, left-handed throw.

"No leaving your chair!" Ashley yelled at him.

Lauderdale plopped back into his chair.

Across the table from Flynn, Cocky had skidded his chair backward, to get out of the combat.

One bread ball hit Flynn near his right eye; another on his left ear.

"A bread fight," Wahler said. He was crouched over so that his head was below the table surface. "A tradition here."

"Every lunch?" asked Flynn.

53

"No," said Wahler. "Only when they serve stew. Youngest gets to throw first."

Keeping his head down, Wahler began to creep away from the table. "Come on, Flynn. Let's go for a walk."

9

"This all must seem rather odd to you," Wahler said. He and Flynn strolled along the veranda and down the lakeside steps. "It did to me, at first."

"I passed a season at Winchester," said Flynn.

"I don't understand you."

"I understand you."

Slowly, Flynn was leading Wahler on a circumnavigation of the main clubhouse.

Flynn had asked Cocky to get their coats and meet him at Flynn's car.

"The Rod and Gun Club was founded more than a hundred years ago," Wahler said. "Five friends, after graduating from Harvard. They bought this acreage as a hunting and fishing lodge for themselves, a place they could get away from the world, their families, jobs, keep in touch with each other and, I guess, maintain some of their undergraduate spirit."

"Is that the gong?"

Flynn climbed the steps to the back porch.

"Big enough, isn't it?" Wahler said.

It was a thick brass plate three meters in diameter hanging from its own oak frame. A leather-headed mallet as tall as a man stood beside it.

"You can hear it from anywhere on the place," Wahler said.

"Who gets to hit it?"

"Taylor, I believe."

"Must make him regret he has ears."

Flynn peered through the steamy window into the kitchen. He counted six servants inside, all male and all apparently Vietnamese.

"Anyway," Wahler said as they continued their walk around the building, "as time went on the five original friends invited their friends. They brought their sons here, when their sons grew to a certain, non-critical age. The clubhouse grew.

55

Expenses mounted. I think the thing was formalized into a club sometime around the turn of the century."

"And the membership became limited."

"I suppose so."

"To what?"

"I don't know. The original five members, their friends, their sons."

"And it became secret."

Wahler took a deep breath and blew out vapor. "It was a place for them to get away. From their wives and small children. Their offices. Their duties. The public eye. Let their hair down, drink what they wanted to when they wanted to, play poker all night, play their silly, sophomoric games, hunt, fish. To coin a phrase: fart when they want to."

They walked up a grade at the back of the clubhouse.

There a large, round area had been flattened and smoothed. A cement circle had been laid in the ground. Red and yellow stripes crossed in the center of the circle. Lights were sunk into the ground, their heavy glass covers flush with the surface of the ground.

"Odd, isn't it," Flynn commented, "how much a helicopter pad can be made to look like a hex symbol?"

To one side a huge earth satellite communications dish appealed to the southwest sky.

"That dish can pull in signals from almost anywhere," Wahler said.

Flynn smiled. "Modern magic."

Down to their left another big area had been cleared and arranged as a skeet-shooting range.

"And down there," said Flynn, "a place of symbolic sacrifice. Clay pigeons."

"What I notice," Wahler said, as they continued their stroll, "is that these men, in building and maintaining this place, in coming here, are trying to recapture their own youths. But look what they recapture. Not their home environments. All of them being upper-class, they really didn't know their homes. They've recaptured, or rebuilt, their lives in boarding schools and summer camps."

"Locks on the refrigerator doors," said Flynn. "I'll bet they have boxes of cookies hidden in their rooms."

"Poor D'Esopo," Wahler said. "Clearly not well brought up. Thought he could go to a kitchen in the middle of the night and find something to eat.

"I find it all sort of sad," Wahler continued. "This is still the only home most of these men have. The only place they don't have to be buttoned-down examples to their communities." Flynn ran his eye over Wahler's striped shirt, rep tie and three-piece suit. "One member," Wahler continued, "a world-famous composer, conductor, a darling of society in every capital in the world, comes here, says very little, never touches the piano, slops around in muddy boots. Every morning he goes out with a big axe and just knocks down trees. Sunup to sundown. No pattern; no point to it at all. He doesn't even trim the trees. Just chops them down. He's devastated acres. Wouldn't you say that's fairly eccentric behavior?"

"We're all true dialectic systems," said Flynn. "Even I have raged at the moon. You, too, I expect."

Wahler laughed. "Once, at my apartment, I strangled a lampshade with my necktie. In the morning I couldn't figure out what I had done or why I had done it. I just knew I had done something that felt good." He laughed again, and said more quietly. "'Once!' It was only three weeks ago."

"I would think," Flynn said slowly, "that The Rod and Gun Club, however secluded and exclusive it is, would be a ripe orchard for any harvester with blackmail on his mind."

Wahler did not respond.

On the north side of the building, a bandy-legged older man was walking toward them. His face was weathered, peculiarly lifeless; his hair thin in patches. His hands were enormous. His boots were muddy and old.

"Hello, Hewitt," said Wahler.

Hewitt's eyes had examined Flynn as they approached each other. The face, the eyes were now averted from Wahler and Flynn.

He nodded.

"This is Flynn," Wahler said. "Hewitt. He's been the club's hunting and fishing guide forever."

57

The man nodded again and continued walking.

"Hewitt's a mute," Wahler said.

"But he can hear?"

"Perfectly. It's sometimes hard to remember. He hears better than most people. Originally, most of the servants here were mutes."

"Now they're Vietnamese. Do any of them speak English?"

"Some. Not very well."

"Ah," said Flynn. "Peace and quiet."

"You've got the idea."

Flynn said, "Meetings happen here."

They had come to the driveway in front of the clubhouse.

"Yes," Wahler said slowly. "Meetings happen here."

"Decisions are made here."

In an overcoat, Cocky stood beside the station wagon. Over his right arm was Flynn's bulky overcoat.

"Yes," Wahler said even more slowly. "Decisions are made here."

"Well," said Flynn, getting into his coat. "Cocky and I are going for a ride. Find a widow and hear about the recently deceased. If the guard at the gate gives us any trouble," said Flynn, "I'm liable to give him what passes for conversation at a board meeting of The Anarchy Society."

Wahler put his hand on Flynn's forearm. "You are coming back, Flynn."

"Sure." Flynn unlocked his car. "I want to discover who shot holes in Oland's new waterproofs."

10

No one was in the reception area of the lounge when they entered Timberbreak Lodge.

"I've seen broccoli farms that do a bigger business than this place," Flynn muttered.

Cocky following him, Flynn went around the reception desk and, without knocking, pushed open the door marked "Manager Private."

"There, Cocky," said Flynn. "There's your switchboard."

The three women sitting at their switchboards looked around at them. They were docilely surprised, as cows are at seeing someone standing in their pasture.

There were switchboard stations for five operators.

Carl Morris came through the door from his office like an offended bull.

"This area's private," he said.

"I should think so," said Flynn. "All these telephone lines for such a wee lodge would make even Maid Marian think twice."

"Oh, it's you, Flynn. I mean, Inspector Flynn. Who's this?"

"Shake hands with Carl Morris, Cocky. The manager of this bustling hostelry."

On the drive down from The Rod and Gun Club Flynn had told Cocky all the facts as he knew them, as well as one or two conjectures.

"You might as well come inside." Morris went into his small office. "You understand. Some press came by earlier. At first I thought you were more of the same. Mister Wahler has said I can talk to you."

"Ah," said Flynn, looking around the closet-sized office as if it were The Hall of Mirrors. "This is where it all happens. Conventions are planned, pillowcase designs are considered, salad chefs hired and fired. Fascinating it is, to see the nerve center of one of the world's grand hotels."

Morris had closed the door behind them. "Sorry I can't ask

you to sit down . . ." The only chair was behind the small desk. "Don't get many guests."

"Do you get any guests?" Flynn asked.

Morris sat on the corner of the desk. "Only those we can't turn away. The occasional lost hunter, or stuck traveling salesman."

"And they don't stay long."

Morris shrugged. "We don't have any food service. No breakfast room. No bar. No ice machines. No swimming pool, sauna, or much hot water."

"Not much repeat trade, I dare say."

"If travelers insist, we rent them a cold bed for overnight and see them off early in the morning."

" 'Insist?' " .

"We turn the 'No Vacancy' sign on every night."

"You've built a bad little business here. Was it much work?"

Morris chuckled. "Think I should write a book, *Reverse Management*?"

"You might try it. More people fail in business than succeed. They might benefit from instruction."

"It's my job. I'm a hired employee."

"Of The Rod and Gun Club."

"You know it."

"This packing case with no motel inside is simply a front for the far grander, more obscure establishment up the road."

"The members have to say where they're going, leave a number. So they say they're going to Timberbreak Lodge. People call here. The ladies out there answer the phone saying Timberbreak Lodge."

"And the calls are transferred to the members' rooms at The Rod and Gun Club."

"Yes. And when someone shows up here looking for one of the members, you know, a reporter, a lawyer, a difficult family member, someone like that, we say he's out walking."

"And the member comes down and meets the person here."

"Right. Years ago, some reporter got hold of the Club's phone number and called a member. That was okay; it had happened before. But the reporter got curious about The Rod

60

and Gun Club, what it was, exactly where it was, who its members are. To make a long story short, a very vague article appeared in *Eyebill* saying such a club exists, where powerful men get together — men whose interests otherwise don't seem to connect — and hunt and fish out of season. And commit other various crimes — such as leaving their wives at home."

"So other journals, more distinguished and thorough than *Eyebill,* became curious."

"Yes. Of course. They sent up reporters and photographers and found Timberbreak Lodge."

Flynn scanned the sagging belly of the office's plywood ceiling. "The building looks like it was ordered in one piece from a factory in New Jersey."

"Very nearly was. The members knew the *Eyebill* reporters were snooping, so they had a little time to get Timberbreak slapped together. We do have running water, and some of it is even in the pipes."

"Build in haste, repent in leisure," said Flynn. "In God we trust."

"Ever since then, when the press gets curious and sends one or two up to snoop around, The Rod and Gun Club sends a few of its younger, less prestigious members down Friday, Saturday nights in hunting clothes, hunting and fishing licenses prominently pinned to their jackets, to sit around the lounge with six-packs of beer, yucking it up, and the press gets tired of watching them and goes away." Morris ran his fingers through his thinning blond hair. "That's how Timberbreak Lodge, The Rod and Gun Club at Bellingham, came to be. Sounds fancy enough, doesn't it?"

"And you?" asked Flynn.

"I was born in the local hospital," Morris said. "That's how I came to be."

"Why are you spending your life running an empty lodge?"

"I was a science teacher in the local regional high school." Morris studied the back of his hands in his lap. "There was a school budget cutback. The Bellingham town fathers decided they wanted to educate their kids for Bellingham, not for the world at large. I was fired. Wife, kids, family here. Not really educated for the world at large, either. What was I supposed to do, go out and cut timber?"

"Honest men do."

Morris looked slapped. "What am I doing that's so dishonest? I'm getting paid to run an empty motel. So I'm running an empty motel. Is that a crime?"

"You're earning a big bonus this weekend, I think."

Morris' right hand cracked the knuckles on his left hand. "Nothing quite like this has ever happened before." He stood up and went around his desk. Opened face-down on the desk was Bruno Bettleheim's *Surviving and Other Essays*. "That's a different world up there on the hill, Inspector. The members of The Rod and Gun Club aren't from around here. And, honest, I only know who a few of them are. God knows who they are. I see the limousines and the helicopters come and go." He stabbed his finger at the closed door. "And I know how many calls a week the various members get from The White House. From Ottawa. From Mexico City. From the heads of the security and commodity exchanges. Senate chambers. Even the Supreme Court, for Christ's sake. I'm supposed to say 'No' to all that?" He sat on the wooden swivel chair behind his desk. "Those guys up there can do what they want to do. That's clear enough. In this world, we're all equals, Inspector Flynn, but some are more equal than others. I think you've heard that. *When the gods on Olympus want to play/Who are we, mere mortal men, to say, Nay?*"

Flynn was looking at the man who looked too big behind his little, empty desk. "And if it comes to it, man, will you perjure yourself? Will you stand up in court and lie?"

"I'm told it won't come to that. Mister Wahler says you, Inspector Flynn, will see to it that it doesn't."

"I will, will I?"

"I've shown reporters around today, walked them through 'the evidence,' played the good old country boy role, clucked with them over an ever-so-tragic hunting accident."

"And they swallowed it?"

"They just wanted to shoot film, grab a story, any story, and get back to someplace warm. Sure they swallowed it. What's to make them suspicious? Why should a country boy like Carl

Morris lie about the death of someone like Dwight Huttenbach? Obviously, there isn't any connection between us."

"And did you tell the same lies to Dwight Huttenbach's widow?"

Morris snorted. "You think she wants to know the truth? She was driven here by a friend, Flynn." Morris laid the palm of his hand flat on the wooden surface of the desk. "A male friend. All these people live and think in a way inconceivable to me. As soon as I opened the door to the room where we had put Huttenbach's things, she backed right away. I doubt she'd even know what belongs to her husband and what doesn't."

"Where is she now?"

"Room 11. Behind the fireplace. She's waiting for the Shaws to pickle her husband in preservatives and pack him in a box. She never even asked to see him."

"We'll go talk to her," said Flynn.

Carl Morris stood up behind his desk. "You ask us to care that some spoiled kid choked on his silver spoon last night? Well, I don't care. The spoons at my house may be aluminum but I need 'em to feed my kids. Doesn't that make sense to you?"

"Yes, it makes sense," said Flynn. "It makes so much sense, regretfully, it even makes a fence four meters high make sense."

11

Flynn knocked on the door of Room 11.

"Who is it?" inquired a woman's voice.

Flynn did not answer.

Presently the door was opened by a short man in his early thirties wearing a well-cut jacket and slacks. His moustache was pencil-thin.

"Yes?"

He did not resist Flynn and Cocky entering the room.

A woman in her late twenties, tailored suit, sat with a straight back, crossed ankles, in one of the two plastic chairs in the room. On the table between the two chairs were used coffee cups.

"Carol Huttenbach, I'm Inspector Flynn. I'm with the police. This is Detective Lieutenant Concannon."

"I'm Max Harvey," said the man coming around from behind them, returning to the other chair. "I drove Carol up."

"You have my sympathy, Mrs. Huttenbach."

"Thank you. I suppose I could ask you to sit on the beds." Her hands were clasped in her lap. "This place is so frightfully cold."

"I must say," drawled Max Harvey, "when I talked to Chief of Police Jensen I didn't get the impression his staff is so grand as to include an inspector and a detective lieutenant."

"You'll be going back today?" Flynn asked.

There was no luggage visible in the room.

"Yes. The children...We're just waiting for the undertakers...."

"I understand."

"The manager put us in this room to get us away from the press."

"Did you talk to the press at all?"

"I did." Max said, as if it were a joke. "As a friend of the family."

"What's there to say?" Carol Huttenbach's voice was low and shivering. "A terrible hunting accident...."

Standing halfway across the small, dark room, Flynn kept his hands in his overcoat pockets. "Why don't you tell me anything you can."

"Why don't you tell me anything *you* can, Inspector," Carol said sharply.

"Carol. . ." Max said.

Flynn waited for a moment, waited for questions which would reveal her contempt for what she had been told, what she had been shown.

Instead, her eyes sought neutrality in the farther wall.

"Just general things," Flynn urged, "about your husband."

"He's dead," she said angrily.

"Did he come here often?" Flynn asked.

"Yes. Often. To this dump. This freezing dump. Packed up his damned guns and fishing rods and woolens and waders and came up here. To this. . .place! Timberbreak Lodge: The Rod and Gun Club. Look at it! Not even a place for us to get a sandwich!"

"This is your first time here?"

"Of course. And last."

"Your husband always came alone?"

She looked at Max a moment, sighed, and shook her head.

"It's all right, Carol."

"You don't believe your husband was alone, Mrs. Huttenbach?"

Carol Huttenbach started to say something, and stopped.

"It's all right, Carol," Max Harvey repeated. "Inspector Flynn is not from the press. He's a policeman. And he knows if he repeats what you say, to the press, he's in trouble. That right, Flynn? They have to know things before we go. Better to be frank with them, than to be dragged back to this. . .God-awful place."

Flynn waited, unsure of the source of her anger.

Cocky sat on the bed nearer the door.

"Where is she?" Carol Huttenbach blurted.

"Where's who?" Flynn asked.

"My God," she sputtered. "It's a man's world, all right, isn't it? The hotel manager —"

"Carl Morris," Max Harvey said.

"That sheep-dipped town cop—"

"Chief Jensen," Max Harvey said.

"You two. You tell me Dwight went outside in the middle of the night to clean his gun and the gun discharged and blew the top of his head off. That can happen to anybody. Especially Dwight, so cocksure of himself he was as careless as a pampered two-year-old. What did you *men* do with the woman he was with? Just send her packing in the middle of the night? Just because Dwight was a man and you're all men and ho-ho-ho, men will be men, belly up to the bar, boys, no need to mention he was with a woman, just pack her off before the little wife gets here?"

Flynn turned slightly, looked at Cocky, then at Max Harvey, then back at Carol Huttenbach. "What makes you think he was with a woman?"

"My husband was never *not* with a woman, Inspector Whatever-your-name-is."

"Ghote." Flynn smiled. "Ghote-dipped."

"My husband was a profoundly spoiled man," Carol Huttenbach announced. "Sexually spoiled. He was boyishly handsome, healthy, rich, powerful, utterly charming, and as sexy as a magazine cover. He didn't even have to blow that damned trumpet of his to have a parade of women following him."

Max Harvey sat forward and put a hand on her arm. She waved it off.

He continued to sit forward, holding his own hands.

"Dwight always had everything his own way. He really believed all the attention he got, all those women throwing themselves at him, were his God-given right."

Often Flynn had seen bereavement express itself as anger at the deceased. Watching Carol Huttenbach, Flynn wondered if he wasn't seeing just plain anger.

"Why can't we ask her what happened? Why did he go outside in the middle of the night to clean his gun?"

"Because someone was in his bed," Max Harvey said with certainty. "Asleep."

Flynn said: "Who?"

"Oh, come on," Carol Huttenbach scoffed. "Don't give me the ho-ho-ho bit. Some of us sweet little things have to put on stupidity publicly, but that doesn't mean privately we're stupid."

"But whom do you think he was with?"

"You tell me."

"I mean," said Flynn. "Do you think he was with anyone in particular?"

"Don't tell me he came to this fabled resort for the cuisine. Of course, with someone in particular. This is pretty far outside his own congressional district, wouldn't you say?"

"But who?" Flynn persisted gently.

"God! Any one of a dozen, I can think of. That female lawyer from Washington. His cousin, Wendy. They could never keep their hands off each other. That female pilot forever flying in from Wyoming, what's her name, Sandy —"

"Wilcomb," said Max Harvey.

"Mark Brandon's wife, at every dinner party, always all over him. Jenny Clifford."

"Quite a jar of worms," intoned Max Harvey, drawing on his king-sized cigarette.

"Jenny Clifford? Does she have a brother?"

"I think so."

"Her brother," said Max Harvey, "is Ernest Clifford, who, at a very young age indeed, is a chief news executive at UBC."

"I see."

Carol Huttenbach said, "Dwight could have gone straight to the top. Straight to The White House. He had money, looks, friends, important connections. He had a magical way of getting things done, getting what he wanted. No one ever understood how he did it. With no apparent effort, no work. All he had to do was pick up a phone, and *kazam!*" Her tone continued angry. "He was so cocksure of himself, he blew his stupid head off."

"And you," Flynn asked. "Would you have gone straight to the top with him?"

"Of course." She crossed her ankles more tightly. "I have the children to think of."

●

12

"Love is not all that's blind." In the parking lot of Timberbreak Lodge, Flynn watched his dashboard gauges work. "Needs gasoline," he said. "Let's go see if Bellingham has a center."

As they slowly went downhill on the black-top road, Cocky said, "Didn't know Ernest Clifford is a news executive at UBC."

"And has a sister attracted to the recently deceased married man." Sunlight poured through the breaks in the clouds. The valley and mountainsides to their left now were colorful under the waning fall foliage. "Ach, that's the way this place is meant to be seen, I'm sure. I told you you might enjoy a few days in the country, Cocky. Peace. Quiet. Dry French toast and bland venison stew. Playful companions. Bodies being dragged about in the small hours."

"Edward Buckingham," said Cocky, "is currently out of office as governor of the state whose border is only fifteen hundred kilometers to the northwest of us."

"Is that so? Thought I'd seen his face in the who-else-is-news columns."

"Elected twice, the limit for that state in succession. Must wait a term before he can run again. Generally believed still to be running the state through his attorney general, now serving as governor."

"Good thing it is, too, that one of us reads the newspapers. Frankly, I find the newspapers' daily announcements of the imminent end of the world seldom right."

"Philip Arlington is a banker, mostly," Cocky said. "Currently serving as a White House economic advisor. I think he taught economics once at Yale, or some such place."

"Unusual for a banker to be so vain."

"I noticed the chin tucks, too. Cosmetic surgery on his face and more than once, I'd say. Not everyone, Frank, ages as gracefully as I do." Cocky chuckled.

"Wendell Oland is senior partner in a major law firm,"

Flynn said. "You may think he's senile. I think he had a genuine regard for his new waterproofs."

"He must have a high regard for all his wearing apparel. At least he keeps all his clothes put safely away somewhere."

"And Lauderdale is a judge," said Flynn. "I'm sure there's no sexual bias in his court. Can't matter to him at all whether a defendant is wearing trousers or a skirt."

"I don't know who Ashley is. Some kind of a businessman, I guess. In financial hot water."

"Maybe he counts Timberbreak Lodge among his assets. And Wahler is Rutledge's lawyer, mind you, not his secretary or driver. And three weeks ago, he strangled a lampshade with his necktie. Indeed, we're all dialectical."

Flynn pulled into a one-pump station. "Fill the tank with your best," he said to the attendant. "Vanilla, if you have it."

"All out of vanilla," said the attendant. "You want chocolate or strawberry?"

"Damn," Flynn muttered to Cocky. "All the wrong people are running the world."

He followed the attendant to the back of the station wagon. "Nice day."

"Seen better. Last July fourth was better. Didn't rain. Next July fourth will be better, too."

"It won't rain then, either?"

"Gas station will be closed then, too." The attendant had a spot of skin cancer on his cheek. Flynn wondered if the man knew what it was he was shaving around every day.

"That always makes for a nice day."

"Except Christmas. My aunt comes Christmas. Hate my aunt."

"But the gas station's closed."

"Wish it were open. Could avoid my aunt."

Flynn waved to the high land to the northwest. "Must be real nice up in that area on a day like this."

"Must be." The attendant put the nozzle back in the pump.

"Are there roads up there?"

"Probably."

69

"Never got up there, eh?" Flynn read the meter and gave the man money.

"Can't. Some sort of secret government installation."

"Oh, yes?"

"All fenced off. Always has been. Can't go nowhere near it."

"I'm sure some of you young chaps know your way up into that area. Where the holes in the fence are."

"Can't even take a wire-cutter to the fence. All electrified. Guards and dogs behind every bush. Probably going to poison us one of these days. Blow us all up or something."

"Would you mind that much?"

"Not if my aunt goes first. Least I'd die happy."

"Why don't you like your aunt?"

"She owns the gas station."

"Oh. I see."

"Good thing about the installation is people here have to drive around it to get to the county seat. Adds eight miles on to their trip, each way."

"What's so good about that?"

"It means I sell more gas."

"What do you care how much gas you sell if your aunt owns the station?"

"I cheat."

Flynn got back into the car. "Cocky, I'm not at all sure the wrong people are running the world after all."

On their right hand side on their drive back uphill was a rustic tavern. Flynn had notice the sign, "The Three Belles of Bellingham," when they were driving down. The parking lot was nearly filled with cars and small trucks.

"Might be a place for tea and scones." Flynn slowed the car.

"It's a roadhouse, Frank. A gin mill."

"Is it? Then we won't embarrass them by asking for scones."

It took Flynn's eyes a moment to adjust to the dark interior of The Three Belles of Bellingham, despite the neon lighting hanging from the ceiling. At this hour Sunday afternoon, most stools at the long bar were being squatted on. Customers at the bar, all men, were drinking whiskey and beer and yelling at a raised television on which a game of football was being played out for them.

There were two women serving bar, both blond, dimpled, comfortably built, and young.

There were also people stuffed into the booths along the outer wall. Most booths had at least two women in them.

"Let's sit at the bar," Flynn said.

"Not a day away from the wife," Cocky commented, "and he's eyeing the barmaids."

"Hardly my fault," said Flynn. "Do you find Judge Lauderdale that attractive yourself?"

They found two stools at the end of the bar farther from the television.

"Who's winning?" Flynn asked the barmaid.

"The Jets. Six to nothing."

"The Jets are winning," Flynn notified Cocky. "Did you bet on the Jets?"

"I bet on the Patriots."

"The Patriots aren't playing the Jets." On the barmaid's full blouse letters spelled out "A l i c e."

"That must be why he bet on them," Flynn said. "What will you have, Cocky?"

"Jameson's," Cocky said. "Water. No ice."

"And you, sir?"

Flynn considered the question. "I had a drink once. Didn't like it much."

Alice laughed, then thought Flynn might be serious. "Nothing for you?"

"You don't carry herb tea, I suppose?"

"Who's Herb?"

"I'll pay for him," Flynn said. "That will justify my use of the stool."

When the barmaid brought Cocky his Irish whiskey, Flynn asked her, "Where's the third?"

"You only asked for one."

"The third belle of Bellingham."

"Oh. Home taking care of our kids. Getting dinner."

71

"Three sisters, are you?"

"Yup."

"And how do you come to own such a place as this, as young as you are?"

"Dad died and left it to us. Nice of him, uh?"

"Very nice."

"Jacques Crepier, the hockey player. Remember him?"

"Died young, I think."

"You could say that. Old, though, for a squash that had been cracked as often as his head had. Don't know how he made it to thirty-eight. Sure you don't want to try another drink, Mister?"

"I'll contribute to the pollution by smoking." He showed her he was filling his pipe. "What's The Rod and Gun Club?" Alice had been about to turn away. "We noticed a little sign on a dirt road as we were coming down."

"It's a private club," Alice said.

"Do they welcome tourists?"

She smiled. "Not even you, handsome." She began to rinse a few glasses beneath the bar. "It's a private, rich man's club. It's always been there."

"Pretty big?"

"Takes up a lot of acres."

"Someone said it's really a secret government installation."

"Who said that?"

"The young man at the gas station."

"Oh, you mean that Herb. He was sent home from school in first grade and never came back. Nobody but idiots believe that. Just 'cause there's a fence around it, and guards. Some of the guys get angry, once in a while, when the huntin' gets slim around here, that they can't go on the rich men's private reserve. Say they're going to take it by storm, or set a fire on it, or something. They never do. That's all just Saturday night talk."

Cocky appeared to be enjoying his Jameson's.

"Must provide lots of local jobs, though. Big place like that."

"I've never known anyone to work there. Guess they get all their help from New York. We never even see anybody from

72

there. They must have their own stores and bowling alley and everything. Once in a while big cars go through town on the way there. Nope." She shook water out of a glass. "It just sits there like a big black hole in the landscape."

A roar went up. The men at the bar all were yelling, beating their fists on the bar. A beer bottle got knocked over. People in the booths were stamping their feet.

"Jets twelve," Alice said.

Money changed hands on the bar, just dimes and quarters. Everyone quietly watched the point-after kick. Much less of a yell; much less money changed hands.

"Least they made one." Alice looked uncertainly at Cocky. "You here for the hunting?"

"We are here for hunting," Flynn said. "Yes."

"You can stay at Timberbreak Lodge. That also calls itself a rod and gun club. Basking in reflected glory, I guess."

"We passed it on the way down," Flynn said. "Is that a good place?"

Alice laughed. "No. People say it's terrible. Sometimes salesmen escape and come in here for a morning warm-up drink. Get the chill out of their bones. They say they don't know how it operates as a motel at all. Cold. The wind whistles right through it. No food, no bar. They change the sheets after you arrive. Mister Morris — I had him for science at the high school? — he owns the place. What he don't know about running a business! The place was built in about a week. He must do some business, though. Every time I drive by it at night the no vacancy sign is lit."

"Alice!" a man called from up the bar. "You're forgetting your old friends!"

"Coming," she said, wiping her hands on a bar rag. "He wasn't a very good science teacher, either. He gave me a passing grade, and I don't even know what the Third Law is."

"Increasing disorder," Flynn advised, "which we must forcefully resist."

"Is that it?"

"Alice! Your Cousin Joe wants a drink! So do I, while you're at it."

73

Alone at the end of the bar with Cocky, Flynn said: "It works. I'll be damned if it doesn't."

"Money can buy anything," Cocky said. "Even privacy."

"Even secrecy," Flynn said. "Is there a difference?"

Cocky's empty glass was on the bar.

"Want another?" Flynn asked.

Cocky shook his head.

"Better get back, then. I need to call Grover and find out all he hasn't done."

The rifle shot sounded very close to the car.

Flynn's car had just been let through the gate in The Rod and Gun Club's fence, gone a short way up the road, and around the curve down to the left.

Flynn stopped the car. "Must say I'm curious. You coming?"

Scraping his left foot behind him through the fallen leaves, Cocky followed Flynn into the woods.

"No shooting!" Flynn bellowed. "We're here!"

Flynn saw the fence through the woods. After a few more steps he saw a man crouching near the fence.

A young doe was on the ground. Her head was near the fence, facing down the length of her body. From the disturbed leaves around the body it was clear the young animal had thrashed painfully.

A bullet hole was behind the deer's right ear.

Hewitt looked up at Flynn. The rifle was propped on the deer's haunch.

Hewitt's eyes were long and dark.

Cocky came up behind Flynn.

"She break her neck on the fence?" Flynn asked.

Hewitt nodded.

A rifle under his arm, the guard walked along the fence from the gate.

"Pretty little animal," Flynn said. "Newborn in the spring."

Standing now, Hewitt slipped his rifle barrel downward under the belt of his coat and tightened the belt.

74

He waved the guard away.

Kneeling between the doe's front and hind legs, he lowered his head almost to the ground. He lifted the doe's stomach onto the back of his neck.

Hewitt stood on bandy legs, the doe slung around his shoulders. The doe's head swung freely.

"I have the station wagon on the road," Flynn said.

Carrying the doe, her head bobbing unnaturally, Hewitt walked away from them, up through the woods, away from the road.

13

"It's the best solution we have," Arlington was saying in a low, conversational tone. "After much consultation."

"And you expect me to accept it?" Ashley's voice was tart.

"No," said Lauderdale. "I expect you to continue being stupid and self-destructive."

Cocky had gone upstairs.

Flynn thought he would take the quiet moment to explore the clubhouse. As he drove up he had heard the firing from the skeet shooting range and presumed all the members were out.

In the long corridor running from the front hall to the dining room at the rear of the building he had heard the low voices talking. He stopped on the forest green carpet.

A door to a room left of the corridor was slightly ajar.

Flynn could not see into the room, but he could hear.

Rutledge asked, "Do you have any other solution, Ashley? We've been waiting a long time."

"And I've tried just about everything."

"You haven't tried getting out of the way," said Lauderdale. "When you saw the company going downhill like a rock you could have let us know. I've got a lot of money invested in you. I've got my kids to think about! I'm about to be a grandfather!"

"I'm sorry about your kids," Ashley retorted. "I don't quite see them in the breadline."

"What's wrong with this concept?" Arlington's voice was strained patience. "You merge your company with Castor Small Arms —"

"I've tried to discuss merger with them."

"At terms impossibly favorable to yourself, I'm sure," Lauderdale scoffed. "Be realistic."

"It's your only way of avoiding disaster," Arlington said. "And I'm not the only one who thinks so. Plus, there are your foreign contracts which Washington wants to see fulfilled."

"I've prostrated myself before Castor," Ashley said. "They won't talk merger with me on any terms."

76

"They'll talk if we want them to," Rutledge said.

"Yes?" Ashley's voice challenged. "Just how do you expect to carry that off?"

"With a phone call," Rutledge answered. "Their biggest small arms plant now is in Wyoming. Fairly isolated. It can be explained to them we foresee difficulties in fuel deliveries in that area..."

"Oh."

Arlington laughed. "That will get them to the negotiating table."

Wahler said: "They'll read that as a threat to sabotage their biggest plant with no fuel or bad fuel."

"I don't even know why we're talking to Ashley," Lauderdale said. "Take the company away from him, and then talk merger."

"Be fair," Arlington said. "In fact, Ashley extended credit to certain Latin American parties at the behest of the United States government. It is their failure to pay that has, shall we say, interrupted Ashley's cash flow."

"Ashley made the decision," Lauderdale charged. "He could have gotten guarantees from somewhere."

"They're putting me out of business."

"You're doing it to yourself."

"Your company is an important American resource," Arlington said. "Besides, some of my banks are carrying your paper. Too much of it."

"I want Ashley out," said Lauderdale.

The sound of the gong, struck once, reverberated throughout the house.

Flynn missed the next thing said.

"Sauna's warm," said Rutledge. "Sauna time."

Flynn backed down the corridor.

"I want Ashley out, whatever happens," Lauderdale repeated. "If there's to be a merger, I don't want Ashley to have any position in the merged company. Or he'll destroy that, too."

"For God's sake, Lauderdale," Ashley said. "What do you know about anything?"

77

"I'll tell you what I know," Lauderdale said waspishly. "I know how to get Ashley-Comfort Incorporated hauled before the courts."

Backing around the corner into the front hall, Flynn heard Arlington groan. "Oh, my God."

14

"I've seen this before." Angled off his huge chest and shoulders, Flynn's small head was poised over the portable chess set in his room.

He moved Black Pawn to Queen Four.

Cocky took his Pawn.

"At its most avuncular, it's called an old-boy network. At its most insidious, a cabal." Flynn moved his knight to King Bishop Three. "A group of people not commonly believed to be connected with each other associating secretly with each other as a means first, of protecting themselves, and then, of advancing their own interests through surprising and oblique uses of power. They may not know what's best for the world, or care, but they know what's best for themselves."

Cocky moved Bishop to Knight Five. "Check. You said you wanted to call Sergeant Whelan."

"Hate the thought of it."

Flynn moved his Pawn to Bishop Three. Cocky took his Pawn. Flynn took Cocky's Pawn with his Pawn.

Cocky moved his Bishop to Bishop Four.

Flynn said, "Guess I better call Grover."

The gong sounded. Even on the second floor of the clubhouse the noise made Flynn's head rock.

"It can't be the dinner hour yet," said Flynn.

He went to the window. The lawn between the clubhouse and the lake was floodlit. All naked, moving at various paces (Clifford ran, whooping; Buckingham and Arlington jogged; Lauderdale took long strides; Oland small steps; Rutledge and Roberts moved at a sedate pace, talking; Ashley moved slowly, a towel over his shoulders; D'Esopo, head down, plopped along behind) the members, red from the sauna, went down the lawn and splashed in the lake. For the first time, Oland and Lauderdale looked natural to Flynn.

"Now's your chance to see your Commissioner in the-altogether-least-he-ever-wore," Flynn advised Cocky from the window. "Something to remember when you have to sit through his long after-dinner speeches."

Cocky did not move.

"Ach, well," said Flynn. "I hope they have a heart specialist somewhere on the place."

He picked up the phone, dialed seven, and then his office number.

Through the window he watched the men outside.

"Grover? Did you have a nice lunch?"

Waist deep in the lake, Buckingham hit Clifford on the back of the head, seemingly hard, with the heel of his hand. Clifford fell forward into the water.

"I would have gone home, except you said you'd call. I was giving you another five minutes."

"Generous of you."

"It's Sunday."

"And you didn't work Wednesday, Thursday, or Friday. I marked the lack of strife in the office."

"Wednesday I spent all day on the Eats Committee."

Clifford regained his feet three meters from Buckingham. He did not turn around. He climbed out of the lake and started back for the clubhouse.

"How do you feel about Sloppy Joes, Inspector?"

"Never felt about one."

"You kidding? I'm talking about Sloppy Joes."

"Grover, I never kid. And I seldom know what you're talking about."

"Sloppy Joes. You know, they're a kind of eats. Do you think you'd like them?"

"No."

"Why not? A lot of guys on the committee do."

"First, because they sound sloppy. Second, because they sound like they're Joe's. You might consider tripe, though."

"What's tripe?"

"What you're talking. Anything important done?" asked Flynn. "You know who killed the old man on the bicycle? You've made a good arrest?"

80

The members had spent very little time in the cold water. They were slogging up the lawn.

"I've found out as much as I can for now. The deceased is a jeweler named Hiram Goldberg. He was seventy-two years old. His wife said he rode his bicycle to work every day but Saturday."

"He was killed Saturday night."

"Will you wait a minute?"

"Sorry. Didn't mean to rush you." Outside, the floodlights went off. "Take your time. Indeed, do."

"Fridays he rode to work, then walked to temple."

"Of course."

"Saturday nights he'd walk from his temple to his office, pick up his bicycle and ride it home."

"Of course. After sundown. After dark."

"So he could bicycle to work Monday morning."

"I see. This Saturday was he carrying any jewelry, any gems on him?"

"He wasn't even carrying money. No wallet even. No identification. That's why I didn't know who he was this morning."

"Oh, that's why."

"Dead on arrival at Boston City Hospital. Not a rich man, I gather."

"And the car that hit him?"

Flynn heard Grover shuffling papers. "Seven cars were reported stolen within the City of Boston after eight-fifteen Saturday night."

"That many? Good grief. Someone should speak to the police about all this. You can't be doing your job, Grover."

"I'm doing my job."

"Indeed you are," said Flynn. "All the above information you got with a single phone call. What was the result of your second phone call, this one to the Vehicular Squad?"

Grover licked his wound a moment. He could not deny Flynn's cutting remark.

"Three cars have been recovered. One was recovered at

81

three a.m. on Lansdowne Street occupied by fourteen year old boys. The operator was charged and released in the custody of his parents."

"Truly stolen."

"The second was discovered outside a doctor's house in Brookline."

"Gunshot victim, do you suppose?"

"The doctor says he doesn't know how the vehicle got there. His wife called Brookline Police at nine o'clock this morning asking the vehicle be taken away."

"Why?"

"It was a hearse, Inspector."

"Ah, yes. Doctors' wives are always sensitive about their husband's reputations."

"The third was found by officers patrolling Elm Street in the South End at noon today. Routine license checking. Returned to owner Willard Matson, 212 Fairview, also South End."

"Was Matson's car found within walking distance of Matson's house?"

The gears ground away in Grover's head. "About a mile, mile and a half away."

"That's the car, Grover. That's the one we want. I'll stake your life on it. Was it inspected for bits and pieces of jeweler before it was returned to the owner?"

Flynn heard a page turn.

"It doesn't say."

"I want that car inspected tonight," Flynn said.

"Tonight!"

"I want you to inspect that car tonight, Grover. Personally. If there's anything suspicious about it, I want it impounded, whatever you have to do, to get it inspected properly by forensic tomorrow."

"Frank," Grover sighed. "Why tonight? You know the bowling league meets —"

"Because it's Sunday, Grover. Auto repair shops are closed on Sundays. Tomorrow is Monday. Auto repair shops are open on Mondays."

Another sigh.

"Don't hyperventilate, man. It might put color in your cheeks."

"212 Fairview is not on my way home."

"Tonight it is. I'll call you in the morning."

Flynn went to the chessboard and moved his Bishop to Queen Three.

Again the gong sounded, making Flynn wish he'd left his ears at home.

"That must be for dinner." Flynn sat down across from Cocky. "No hurry, I'm sure."

"Frank?"

"Been thinking, have you?"

"Paul Wahler isn't really one of them, is he? He's not a member of The Rod and Gun Club."

Flynn cast his mind's eye over the men he had just seen duck into the cold lake. Wahler was not one of them.

"Paul Wahler," said Flynn, "is like Timberbreak Lodge. A front. What did the Bellingham belle named Alice say? 'Basking in reflected glory.'"

Cocky castled.

Flynn studied the board. He castled, too.

"Well," said Flynn. "A whole new game. Might as well break for dinner. However fresh the raw materials, I'm sure dinner has been cooked to bland school fare. We should have bought biscuits in downtown Bellingham. That's the trouble with you and me, Cocky. Always thinking of the wrong thing."

15

Cocky limped downstairs while Flynn returned to his room to answer the phone. It had rung just as he was closing his door.

"Timberbreak Lodge," he answered. "Where the elite meet."

"Da? The house is in an uproar."

Not that there was any question in his mind as to who was speaking, Flynn knew "The house is in an uproar" would be spoken only by his nine year old son, Winny. At least, he was sure Winny was the only nine year old who would say such a thing.

"What's wrong, Winny?"

"Well, you see: Randy and Todd have been feeling that Jenny has been spending too much time in the bathroom."

"There are two bathrooms."

"They've been observing that Jenny might be getting too conceited."

"She has every reason to," said the father of the perfect thirteen-year-old daughter.

"They suspect her of practicing facial expressions in the bathroom mirror."

"But they don't know, do they?"

"There's some evidence. Every time she comes out of the bathroom she uses her face like a film star meeting the public. You know, the look-but-don't-touch expression."

"Condescending."

"Yes. Well, I think Randy and Todd decided they didn't like being her public and decided to protest."

"Winny, what did they do?"

"They ran the piano up against the bathroom door."

Flynn could just see his twin teenage sons doing so. Not only doing so, but doing so quickly and quietly.

"Yes?"

"Jenny couldn't get out."

"There's a bathroom window."

"Not very big and high up in the wall. Quite a fall to the ground outside. So Jenny began to shout and scream. She said she was late for swimming practice. Which she was."

"Jenny never lies."

"Then Mother began managing things."

"Good."

"Not good. There was a weak floorboard."

"Oh, no."

"One leg of the piano fell through the floorboard. The piano is stuck against the bathroom door. Jenny inside, crying. Randy and Todd outside, laughing. Mother up and down the cellar stairs, yelling about wires and pipes which might be broken."

"Winny, how did you get this phone number?"

"It was on the pad next to the phone. I thought I should call you. There has to be a solution, Da. This uproar has been going on for almost an hour."

"Can't the boys lift the piano?"

"They say they can't, Da. They've made a big thing of trying although, privately, I think most of their energies have gone into grunting loudly. And laughing."

"Jenny is missing swimming practice because she's stuck in the bathroom because a piano is stuck against the bathroom door?"

"What's the solution, Da?"

"Winny. The solution is perfectly simple."

"What would it be, Da?"

"While you and Randy and Todd are lifting the front end of the piano . . ."

"Yes, Da?"

"Have your mother sit at the keyboard."

"Yes, Da."

"And play something light. Good-bye, Winny."

"Good-bye, Da."

16

"**G**lad to see you didn't dress for dinner," Flynn said to the naked Wendell Oland.

The members of The Rod and Gun Club were having drinks in the Great Hall.

Oland looked at Flynn as does an experienced fish at a purchased fly.

Cocky was nowhere in the room.

Away from the bar table, Ernest Clifford sat alone on one of the leather divans, sipping a beer. He was leafing through the magazine *Country Journal*.

Flynn sat next to Clifford on the divan and enquired easily, "What is your relationship to Buckingham?"

Clifford looked over at Buckingham standing by the bar table, drink in hand, talking with Wahler. "He's my uncle."

"Oh."

"My mother's brother."

"And are you friendly?"

"Sure. Why not?"

Granted, Flynn had seen the incident at some distance, through a window, under artificial light, but Buckingham's hitting Clifford in the back of the head in the lake less than an hour ago had not seemed friendly. The head-down way Clifford had then walked away from Buckingham had not seemed a friendly reaction either.

Sitting next to Clifford on the divan there was little doubt in Flynn's mind the young, tall, broad-shouldered Clifford could have made pudding of the older, fatter Buckingham within a count of thirty.

Dunn Roberts brought Flynn a bourbon and water. "That should whet your appetite, Flynn."

"Thank you, Senator."

After his early-morning fishing expedition, drinking his breakfast, napping through lunch, Senator Dunn Roberts appeared relaxed and affable.

"We haven't had a chance to talk yet, Flynn. Anything I can do . . ."

"One simple question: Where were you last night at eleven?"

"In bed, reading a book. Going fishing early this morning. So went up about nine-thirty. Couldn't sleep. So read. Heard the bang. Came down. Somebody had shot Huttenbach."

"What book?"

"Crozier's *De Gaulle.*"

"Were you in on the decision to move Huttenbach's body?"

Dunn Roberts looked around the room. "Yes."

"Who else was in on the decision to move Huttenbach's body?"

Still looking down the huge room, Roberts said, "Anyone else who says he was."

"I see."

"Anything else?"

"Not right now."

Dunn Roberts picked up an empty ice bucket and brought it to Taylor, who was just leaving the room.

Flynn turned his head back to Clifford. "You have a sister."

"We're a big family, I guess. I have two sisters."

"And one was attracted to Dwight Huttenbach."

Country Journal still open on his lap, Clifford looked directly into Flynn's face. "I guess Jenny was."

"You guess?"

"Jenny has been seen with him. I have heard they showed up at places together. She volunteered for his last campaign."

"Were they intimate?"

Clifford wrinkled the bridge of his tanned nose. "Probably."

"After Huttenbach married?"

"I'd say so."

"Is your sister married?"

"No."

"So how do you feel about your sister's probable intimacy with a married man who happens to be a friend of yours?"

"Like I should blow Huttenbach's head off with a shotgun."

87

More color came to Clifford's face. He shook his head. "Jenny's a grown-up, Flynn. What she does is her business."

"Which do you really feel?"

"Oh, come on."

"Huttenbach had an easy time with women?"

"Not more so than others."

"You mean, not more than you."

"These are easy days, Flynn."

"You're not married?"

"No."

"Do you consider yourself a special friend of Huttenbach's?"

"Not special. We were friends. I liked him—especially when he left his trumpet home. He was really awful on the trumpet. And he thought he was good. I've always known him. Jenny's always known him. If Huttenbach and my sister enjoyed each other, that was their business, not mine."

"What if they didn't enjoy each other?"

"If things worked out badly? I don't know that they did. I've been assigned to the Middle East the last six months, Flynn. I don't know all that much about what's been going on in Jenny's life. I called her last night to tell her that Dwight is dead."

"What was her reaction?"

"She cried. But Jenny always cried when her toys broke."

Flynn sniffed his drink and put it on a side table.

"I have a daughter named Jenny," said Flynn. "Momentarily indisposed."

"Sorry to hear that."

"Nothing a little uplifting music won't solve."

Lauderdale carried two martini glasses over and handed the full one to Flynn. "The man who found my music box."

Tonight, Lauderdale's wig was raspberry in color, but similiarly tilted as the one he'd worn to lunch. His gown was a seedy pink. The material was strained across his chest. The breasts of his gown looked punched in. One strap hung off his right shoulder. The stockings on his thin legs were baggy. His high-heeled shoes looked enormous.

"I see you did dress for dinner," Flynn said. "Almost."

He took the martini and put it on the side table next to the bourbon.

"I recovered the music box," said Lauderdale. "Thanks to you. I'll play it for everyone at dinner. Who do you suppose hid it in the storage room?"

"I understand you have a noted composer-conductor among your membership."

" 'A noted composer-conductor,' " Lauderdale quoted. "That's pretty good. You'd better watch this man, Clifford. With his brains, it won't take him much longer to figure out you shot Huttenbach."

Lauderdale wobbled away on his high heels.

Across the room, D'Esopo was drinking beer from a can.

"You want a clue?" Clifford asked.

"You going to incriminate yourself?"

"You've heard of Ashley-Comfort, Incorporated?"

"They make guns, I think."

Clifford nodded his beer glass toward the member in the hounds-tooth jacket. "That's Ashley. You've heard of the Huttenbach Foundation?"

"Not really."

"It's a humanitarian foundation set up by the Huttenbach family. Gives away millions a year. Of course Dwight sat on its board of directors. The foundation was heavily invested in Ashley-Comfort."

"A humanitarian foundation was heavily invested in a company that makes guns?"

"Right. A couple of weeks ago, the Huttenbach Foundation dumped its Ashley-Comfort stock. It really drilled the final hole in Ashley's sinking ship. And Dwight didn't warn Ashley it was going to happen."

"Are you sure he knew?"

"Of course he knew."

"Why didn't he tell Ashley?"

"Didn't care. Didn't think it mattered. Thought Ashley couldn't do anything about it anyway. Wanted to screw Ashley. Take your pick of the above reasons. The net result is the same:

Ashley swamped. Or, is swamping." Clifford finished his beer. "Not nice. Not quite in the spirit of The Rod and Gun Club."

"And what about you?" Flynn asked. "Is Ernest Clifford heavily invested in Ashley-Comfort?"

Clifford shrugged. "I honestly don't know. You might ask Uncle Buck."

In a blue blazer Rutledge crossed the room, bringing Flynn a Scotch and soda. "Anyone taking care of you, Flynn?"

"I've already had two." Flynn nodded at the two full glasses on the table beside him.

Standing in front of Flynn, Rutledge asked, "Everything all right at home?"

Glass in hand, Flynn asked, "Are you having my calls monitored?"

"Do you think your sons will be able to lift the piano by themselves?"

Clifford looked from one man to the other.

"Can't be too cautious," Rutledge said.

The gong sounded again.

"Ach," said Flynn. "I wish someone would warn me when that damned thing is to go off."

"You've been warned, Flynn." Rutledge turned toward the door into the hallway. "Dinner time."

•

17

Rumble de dump!
Rumble de dump!
Our lake is bottomless!
Our forests wide!
We hunt the hippopotamus!
And skin his hide!

Flynn skidded his chair back from the table and muttered:
"Ye gods and small fishes!"

At the end of each line the members of The Rod and Gun
Club chanted, they banged their empty beer tankards on the
heavy, scarred dining table.

Rumble de dump!
Rumble de dump!
Our friends are many
And our voices loud!
Wives? Haven't any!
We live without cloud!

The members sat at the round table in the same order as
they had at lunch: Oland to Flynn's left, Wahler to his right.
Dunn Roberts sat between Oland and Rutledge.

And Cocky was missing.

D'Esopo did not join in the noise, of course, nor did Flynn.
Wahler smiled and tapped his tankard lightly against the table.

Rumble de dump!
Rumble de dump!
We kill all the deer!
And drink all the beer!
Live without fear!
Sure no one can hear!

Sitting back, hands folded in his lap, Flynn survived
another two stanzas of this noisy drivel which had attained
neither the puerile nor the doggerel, as well as the loud beating
of the tankards against the table.

Across the table, only Ernest Clifford and Edward

Buckingham were laughing as they chanted and banged. Philip Arlington performed the ritual with precision and high seriousness. Thomas Ashley seemed to be doing his duty. To Flynn's right, Robert Lauderdale was chanting in falsetto and getting an extra noise out of his bracelets as he banged his mug. To Flynn's left, Wendell Oland used big gestures, as if he were leading hundreds. Dunn Roberts was hitting the table hardest, and with the edge of his tankard, doing maximum damage to both table and tankard. Charles Rutledge sang and banged with a choirmaster's formality.

Flynn supposed, if this or something like it, was a nightly ritual, then the previous night Dwight Huttenbach had sat among them, in either Flynn's chair or Cocky's, and chanted and banged with them. Each man's characteristics would have been the same; what characteristics would have been Huttenbach's?

There was no reflection, in this evening's ritual of bravado, that, in the interim, one of their members had had his brain pierced by shotgun pellets.

Traditions continue relentlessly, regardless of facts.

Rumble de dump!

Rumble de dump!

When he was certain relative silence would ensue, Flynn pulled his chair into the table.

All were looking at him for reaction.

Mildly, he asked, "Are those beer vessels called tankards?"

"Yes," said Arlington.

"Ever called cans?"

In annoyance, Rutledge said, "I suppose so."

Flynn was silent.

"Why?" asked Roberts.

"Just wondering," Flynn said, "about the origin of the word, *cantankerous.*"

Roberts whooped with laughter.

D'Esopo put his right hand over his eyes.

Taylor and the Vietnamese helper served the dinner of boiled fish and broccoli. If there was anything Flynn disliked more than broccoli, it was boiled fish. Served together, they were Flynn's best idea of missing supper altogether.

He immediately supposed dessert would be tapioca pudding.

Flynn had decided as a boy that if life were only boiled fish, broccoli and tapioca pudding, there would be no culinary reason for living.

Lauderdale started his music box. "You're right, Flynn. *F* is missing."

"Pity the whole thing isn't still missing," said Ashley.

Lauderdale put the music box on the table.

Rutledge asked, "Where's Concannon?"

Flynn said, "He must have detected what is on the menu."

D'Esopo had both hands over his eyes.

"Does anyone know where Concannon is?" asked Rutledge.

"We'll keep a plate warm for him in the kitchen," Taylor said.

"Maybe he didn't hear the gong," Lauderdale giggled.

The music box ran down.

"He says he wants to stay here," Arlington was saying to Clifford, "in the cabin by the lake, until it's time for him to go to the terminal ward. Says there's no place else for him to go. Wife died ten years ago of the same disease. Has a daughter in Vermont somewhere who apparently hates him."

"Can't be anything he said," Buckingham laughed.

"A son serving a long stretch in a prison in Hawaii for some silly thing or other. Some sort of mayhem."

"But will he be able to go out with us tomorrow?" Rutledge asked. "Is he up to it?"

"He wants to," Arlington said. "Wants to keep going until he drops. Hewitt's a tough old bird."

"I saw Hewitt this afternoon," said Oland. "Stomping along lakeside with a doe over his shoulders. Looked perfectly fit to me."

Rutledge said: "We all mean to go deer hunting tomorrow, Flynn. Will you accompany us?"

"Yes," said Flynn. "If you're all going."

"Great!" exclaimed Clifford. "There are plenty of rifles in the storage room, as you know, but after dinner, have a look at mine. I've got —"

"Won't be taking a rifle," said Flynn.

D'Esopo's look at Flynn had settled into permanent dismay.

"Going deer hunting without a rifle?" asked Oland. "Are you one of these bow-and-arrow fans? Or do you mean to slay the deer with your wit?"

"You breed deer here at The Rod and Gun Club, don't you?" asked Flynn.

"Yes," said Buckingham, "And stock the lake."

"And most of you have wives, I think?"

"Yes," said Roberts.

Flynn said into his plate of boiled fish and broccoli: "So much for *rumble de dump.*"

He wondered what the three belles of Bellingham were having for dinner. He thought of his wife's good soup.

Dinner conversation then became a series of narrative monologues, hunting and fishing stories, each bright enough, most showing the narrator in a good light. Clifford's story was personally modest; only Robert's made fun of himself.

As the men at the table made repeated trips to the beer keg with their tankards, the stories became louder, slower, and less credible. Volume fought veracity and won.

Clearly, most of the men at table had heard most of the stories before. Only Oland insisted he had never heard any of them before. Therefore many stories were told despite the obvious boredom of most of the listeners.

When Lauderdale became bored with a story he started the music box again, and again *The Wedding March, F*-less, tinkled through the dining room.

Dessert was tapioca pudding.

Over coffee Dunn Roberts said in a voice well used to calling meetings to order: "I'm hankering to know what D'Esopo, Flynn and his cohort, Concannon, have discovered so far about the death of Huttenbach."

"Commissioner D'Esopo and I will be meeting after this

94

slimming exercise you refer to as dinner," Flynn said. "We have several things to discuss."

D'Esopo put down his beer tankard.

"Can't you tell us anything?" asked Roberts.

"Yes, I can tell you something," answered Flynn. "To a great degree, although not entirely, I have satisfied myself that Huttenbach was not killed by someone outside The Rod and Gun Club. The people in the surrounding area know The Rod and Gun Club exists, or they know there's something up here. I suppose they resent having to drive around it, and resent not being able to hunt and fish through here, that your two thousand acres of timber isn't being farmed, that whatever is here provides no jobs for the surrounding communities whatsoever—except, that is, for Carl Morris, who runs an empty lodge, at least five telephone operators well paid, I suspect, for their tight lips, and the odd gratuity handed out when necessary to such pillars of the community as the Chief of Police and Roads, in this case, at least, the County Coroner, as well as whoever else might be tempted to tell the truth. Whether your power is really all that pervasive, whether your perimeter of guards, dogs and fences is all that perfect, I cannot say, but over a very long period of time, you seem to have gotten everyone to believe in these defensive devices." Flynn banged the cold ashes from his pipe into the brass ashtray.

Arlington smiled at Rutledge, and Rutledge at Oland.

The Wedding March began to tinkle through the dining room again.

"I'm not sure you understand me." Flynn declared his chance at dinner over by standing up to leave. "No one from the village or surrounding area, none of your associates outside The Rod and Gun Club, none of your relations not members of The Rod and Gun Club seems to know you members well enough, or care enough about you, to penetrate your defenses, and do murder."

As Flynn was leaving the room, he heard Clifford's voice say, quietly, *"Rumble de dump!"*

95

18

"I need to know what all this means to you," Francis Xavier Flynn said to Commissioner Eddy D'Esopo. They were in a small, book-lined den with a few reading chairs, a desk. Flynn was sitting while D'Esopo paced. "You were quite right. I don't like it at all. You've put the three of us—you, Cocky, and me—in the way of being accused as accessories to murder after the fact."

"Come on, Frank. We have some positions. We are police."

"Not in this state."

"You do, Frank. Don't you?"

"Is that what you think? Is that why I'm here?"

"I know you've operated well outside my jurisdiction before. And gotten away with it."

Flynn said, "I suppose so. But not the way you think."

D'Esopo squared his shoulders. "I'm just a guest here. However incriminating that may be. And I didn't ask you to bring Concannon. I distinctly told you to come alone. And to shut up about where you were going." D'Esopo waved his hands. "And here your kids seem to feel free to call you, whenever one of them spends too long in the bathroom!"

"Ach," said Flynn. "If Jenny only knew the extent she has to go to, to get a little privacy in this world."

After dinner, Flynn had toured the clubhouse, finally, in a loose search for Cocky. Not in Flynn's room; not in his own.

Flynn had found a communications room at the back of the house with several television screens, several computer consoles, several telephones. In the basement he found a well-equipped gymnasium and the large sauna.

Along the corridor from the great hall to the dining room were three of these smaller rooms overlooking the dark lake. Obviously they were designed for quiet reading, quiet meetings. The largest, in the middle, in which the affairs of Ashley-Comfort Incorporated had been discussed that afternoon, had a baby grand piano in it. `

He had not found Cocky.

"That's all very well, Eddy. But I need to know what all this means to you."

In the room next to them, chords rippled from the piano.

"You're not one of these people. You're not a member. And you never will be. Do you know that?"

Accompanying himself on the piano, Lauderdale began to sing the old romantic ballad, *The Isle of Capri,* in a loud, wavering falsetto.

"That nut!" D'Esopo clapped the palm of his hand to the back of his neck.

Flynn chuckled. If such was Lauderdale's "act," as Wahler had described it, it was funny. Especially when Lauderdale's off-key falsetto and fumbling piano notes only could be heard through the wall, the sight of him sitting alone at the piano in raspberry wig, punched-in evening gown, huge high-heeled shoes working the pedals could be only imagined in the mind's eye. Satiric. For an all-male company, Lauderdale was satirizing what errant people thought of the most terrible traits of womanhood, from constant bitchiness to an insistence on ballads after boiled fish and broccoli. Errant, as satire is, but funny.

"I swear to God!" D'Esopo said.

"As I was saying, Eddy: You're not one of these people. By the way, tonight I might join you in burglarizing the kitchen. Together, we might manage to break a few locks."

In the next room, Lauderdale reached for a high-*C* and missed.

In a more serious tone, Flynn said, "Eddy, I've had enough of this. You asked me to come; you ask me to stay. I cannot take part in destruction of evidence, bribery, suborning of witnesses, possible perjury..."

"I have an expensive child."

Flynn waited, saying nothing.

"Born defective," D'Esopo said. "Born with a defect the very name of which make me sick even to think about, let alone say."

Flynn said, "I didn't know."

"It— My wife and I decided some time ago it was okay,

97

necessary, to call our child an 'it.' You may not think it nice, but
we decided, we had to decide, that referring to *it* as *it* was the
only way of impersonalizing *it*. Staying sane."

Flynn thought of his own five healthy, gorgeous children
and said nothing.

"It needs constant care, twenty-four hours a day, twelve
months a year. More than any man can afford; more than any
mother can manage."

"I'm terribly sorry, Eddy."

"A while ago, when federal and state agencies cut back on
programs caring for such children, our child was turned back to
us. I couldn't afford private care. I have the other kids.
Coincidentally, at about the same time, I was invited up here. I
came quick enough. I was glad to get away for a weekend.
Home had been turned into. . .a kind of hell. Have you ever
heard of the Huttenbach Foundation?"

"Just recently."

"That first weekend I was here, Dwight Huttenbach
mentioned to me that his family foundation runs a school,
hospital, whatever you want to call it for such children. Within
ten days my child was in that hospital, where it has been ever
since. And, honest, Frank, some of its abilities have improved.
The people there are just marvelous."

"And no expense to you."

"Very little expense."

"How did Huttenbach know about your child?"

"In vino veritas," D'Esopo smiled at Flynn. "You and I have
never had a drink together, Frank."

"Maybe I'm missing out on something. Whose guest at The
Rod and Gun Club were you, Eddy? Whose guest are you?"

"Ashley's."

"Ach: guns."

"That's right. Buying guns and ammunition for the force."

Flynn tried to remember. "Do we Boston police use Ashley-
Comfort guns and equipment?"

D'Esopo shrugged. "We were anyway. To answer your next
question, we are not now buying more or less equipment from
Ashley-Comfort than we ever were. I do admit that Ashley

asked me, as Edward D'Esopo, individual, not as Commissioner of Boston Police, to make a quiet endorsement of Ashley-Comfort equipment. And I found, in good conscience, I could do so."

Now Lauderdale was warbling through *Silver Threads Among the Gold*. Oddly, it wasn't funny anymore. Flynn supposed satire must keep its distance from reality to remain funny.

"And what else do you do for the members of The Rod and Gun Club, Eddy?"

"Oh, sometimes the V.I.P. treatment when one of them comes to Boston and asks for it. Lay on a police escort with siren. Special police protection, the few times it's been asked. Had a police honor guard at a funeral for someone's maiden aunt, once. That took a bit of doing. I said she'd baked brownies for the vice squad."

"It would seem to me," conjectured Flynn, "that many of these members would have children and grandchildren at schools and colleges in the Boston area. How many times have you stopped charges against them, Eddy?"

"I'm not going to answer that, Frank."

"And in all this time, I'm willing to wager, no one has put you up for — "

In the next room, Lauderdale's singing stopped for a brief moment. As did the sound of the piano.

Then the keys of the piano were banged.

The falsetto returned and warbled successfully through high-*C*. It became a horrible shriek.

"That guy!" D'Esopo said. "I don't see what's supposed to be so funny — "

D'Esopo read Flynn's face.

"He's just playing," D'Esopo said.

The shriek became a gurgling and a coughing.

Finally, there was a weak yell in a distinctly man's voice.

"Isn't he?" D'Esopo asked.

Flynn said: "I think not."

19

Flynn looked through the porthole in the door into the lit gymnasium.

Dressed only in shorts, Taylor was working a leg press.

Flynn entered.

Taylor stopped his workout and stood up. Throughout his body his muscles were extremely well defined.

"Do you wish to use the equipment, Mister Flynn?"

"Funny time of day, or night, to be taking such heavy exercise."

Taylor shrugged. "It's the only time I'm sure the members don't want to use the room."

Flynn looked up the stairway beside the sauna. Half the bulkhead door was open. "How long have you been exercising?"

"Years," the muscle-bound young man said modestly.

"I mean, tonight."

"Oh. About twenty minutes."

"You're not sweating."

"I'm used to it. I do this every night."

"Why is the bulkhead door open?"

"Fresh air." Even standing easy in all his heavy muscles, Taylor remained the obedient servant, ready to fetch and carry. "Something wrong, Mister Flynn?"

"Yes. I missed you from the music room."

"The music room?"

"The room with the piano in it. Everyone showed up there but you."

"Why? What happened?"

What happened was that when Flynn and D'Esopo hurried into the room, they found Lauderdale slumped over the piano keyboard.

Rutledge was standing over Lauderdale at the piano as if waiting to turn a page of sheet music for him.

Lauderdale's raspberry wig was half off. The left cheek of his face rested on the middle octave. His purple tongue stuck out between teeth which had bitten into it, starting a stream of blood. His eyes bulged as if staring incredulously at the number of upscale notes.

And the door onto the veranda was open.

"Lauderdale's been strangled," said Flynn.

"Dead?"

"Yes," said Flynn certainly. "Dead."

"I heard the noises." Taylor in his taut young flesh was an ironic contrast to the flabby male in his fifties dressed in an evening gown relaxed in death only a few meters away. Flynn figured the music room was right over the gymnasium. "I guess I heard the noises. I thought he was kidding. I mean, I heard the silly noises he was making. He was dying?"

"Without much of an audience," said Flynn.

Buckingham, who had arrived in the doorway of the music room immediately after Flynn and D'Esopo, had shouted, very loudly, "Oh, my God! Oh, my God!"

That summoned Arlington, Clifford, Ashley, then Cocky and Oland. Wahler and Roberts were the last to arrive.

Looking up from his examination of Lauderdale, Flynn asked, "Where's Taylor?"

"Probably in the gym," Clifford said.

And Flynn said to Cocky: "Keep everyone out of here. Try to keep their bloody hands off the evidence this time."

Flynn had run down the basement stairs to the gymnasium.

Now the cold night air from the open bulkhead door was making Taylor shiver.

"How long were you in prison?" Flynn asked.

"How do you know I was?"

"The was society now works," Flynn said. "Society now takes its undesirable citizens off the streets and puts them into prisons with fully equipped gymnasiums and all the time in the world to build themselves up into extremely strong undesirable citizens. Few others have the time to set themselves up muscularly as well as does our criminal class."

"It's the only way to stay alive in prison. It's the only way of working off the pressure. Getting yourself tired enough to sleep. Of protecting yourself."

"I know," said Flynn. "How long?"

"Three years. A little more than three years."

"And which crime was your specialty?"

"Marrying people."

"That's a crime?" asked Flynn. "I've known people to be congratulated for it."

"In my case, they called it bigamy."

"And what's bigamy these days?"

"Getting caught with nine wives."

"Nine! Good heavens, man, you are the marrying kind."

"Judge— The judge who sentenced me said it was a bad habit I should break."

"A bad habit with too much future in it, I'd say. Your mother never told you about divorce?"

"It would always happen too quickly. There would always be so much urging on the part of the in-laws-to-be. I never had the heart to tell them all, well, I'd been married before. Was still married. I'd just get sucked up by another family. Bang, I'd end up at the church rail again."

"Come now, Taylor. You married nine times without fraudulent purposes?"

"I never got anything out of it but the wedding presents. And how many Kitchen Aides do you need? I didn't need any."

"Taylor..."

"I like weddings. I'm crazy about them. Crazy, I guess. I like being the groom. I have everybody's attention. Everybody loves me. I love the in-laws being so glad to see me, always, to have me in the family. I love wedding receptions. I love wedding nights. Doesn't everybody?"

Flynn studied Taylor. Yes, with Taylor's basically good build, clear olive skin, bright dancing eyes, dark curly hair, Flynn could see Taylor being grabbed into any family with a daughter.

He looked like someone who belonged on top of a wedding cake.

Taylor blushed and shivered at the same time. "The prison psychiatrist said I'm badly oversexed. But she was..."

"I know. A female. I'm sure she was very helpful to you."

102

"She diagnosed my problem correctly."

"I'm sure she did."

"That's why I work here, Mister Flynn. To keep myself away from women. I've been out almost nine months and I haven't married once. Haven't even been close to it."

"You've done well, lad. All us fathers of daughters are grateful."

"One is too many," Taylor said miserably. "A million aren't enough."

"At least you know you have a problem," commiserated Flynn.

"Badly oversexed," blushed Taylor. "So I work out every night. Just like in prison. It helps get rid of it."

"And did you and your nine wives spawn many children?"

"Oh, yes," Taylor said happily. "Lots and lots. Nice ones, too. All my in-laws really love them. They were all glad to have them. You know, to take care of them. Obviously, I couldn't."

"I can see you were busy."

"Toward the end there, I was very busy," admitted Taylor.

"You mean, you never abandoned any of these wives?"

Taylor shook his head. "I wouldn't marry a girl and then abandon her. Especially if she was pregnant. Toward the end there, I lost weight. I lost ten, fifteen pounds."

"We each react differently to strain."

"Without exception, all my in-laws were nice. I mean, about taking all the kids. Taking all my wives back. I married into some real nice families. Of course they all did sort of gang up on me, at the end there. You know, they got me dragged into court. But they were all just jealous, you see."

"Jealous over you."

"Yes," said Taylor. "Once word began getting around. You see, a minister recognized me as having been in that same church a few weeks before. As groom. First one father-in-law got angry, then they all got angry."

"I can see they might be touchy on the topic."

"I figure if none of the families could have me," Taylor said shrewdly, "none of the families wanted any of the other families to have me. So they had me put in the clink."

103

"I've often heard," sighed Flynn, "that talent can be a burden."

"It took the three years I was in stir for everybody to divorce me and annul me."

"And who was the judge who sentenced you to celibacy?"

Taylor looked at the ceiling.

"Lauderdale," said Flynn.

"That old hen."

"And was it Lauderdale who got you this sexless job?"

"I didn't want to go into a monastery, Mister Flynn. I don't like cheese all that much. Besides, the prison psychiatrist said I'll calm down with age. I will likely calm down with age, won't I, Mister Flynn?"

"Not," advised Flynn, "if you keep yourself in shape."

20

"Sprightly lad, that Taylor," Flynn said to Cocky as he re-entered the music room. "Who said we all lead lives of quiet desperation? And where have you been the while?"

"I had dinner out."

"Wise man. I didn't have dinner in."

"I took a bottle of Scotch from the bar table and walked down to Hewitt's cabin by the lake. We had fried fish and venison steak together. I brought you back a bag of apples."

"I smelled the fish boiling, too." Flynn, hands on hips, surveyed the murder room. "Didn't think of taking evasive action."

"He's not a well man, Frank."

"I've heard."

"You can see a strange protuberance through his shirt. His skin is more yellowish than weathered, you know what I mean? I think he should be in the hospital."

"And young Taylor is in the basement trying to burn off enough energy for nine people, all of them husbands." Flynn nodded to the bewigged, evening-gowned male corpse collapsed on the piano keys. "And there's a member of the bench who's played his last bar. Have you discovered anything interesting?"

"Strangled by an ordinary piece of used clothesline, knotted at both ends. The murder took some preparation, therefore, but not much. I'd say whoever strangled him was very strong. The clothesline is deeply embedded in his neck. It's possible the neck is broken."

"The murderer didn't hesitate. I mean, he did it quickly, then. No need for him to take a second breath." Flynn got down on his hands and knees on the floor just inside the veranda door.

"Nothing of interest on the veranda visible in this light."

Flynn's head was as nearly at eye-level with the floor as possible. "Where shoes and boots might not leave a mark on a bare floor, sweaty bare feet do."

"Oland?"

Standing, Flynn gauged the distance from the door's threshold to the faded oriental carpet. "But sure, anyone could make that leap. It's hardly more than a step."

"Or the murderer, thinking he might be caught in the room with Lauderdale, could simply have opened the door, to make us think someone had come in and gone out that way. Or just gone out."

"Rutledge was here when we arrived," said Flynn. "And we were just next door."

"You didn't hear anything, Frank?"

"I did. I heard the old boy croaking. At first I thought it was part of his after-dinner act. It wasn't until I heard the distinctly male voice that I realized it was no act."

Cocky said, "I put the apples in your room. And moved my Pawn to Queen Four."

"Pawn to Queen Four, eh? Now, that's interesting." Flynn turned the lock in the door to the veranda. "Does that door to the corridor lock?"

"No."

"Doesn't matter," said Flynn. "Let's get them all in the great hall anyway. I have a few choice words to utter. Don't I just!"

21

"Coffee, Flynn? Or would you prefer a drink?" Rutledge stood by the bar table ready to be helpful.

"A cup of hot water, please." Flynn pulled a tea bag out of his jacket pocket. "And a spoon."

For the number of people in the great hall, the room was uncommonly quiet. The crackling fire seemed a strange postlude to Lauderdale's singing.

D'Esopo sat farthest from the fire, in a deep leather chair against the outside wall. What looked like a stiff drink was balanced on his chair arm. Lighting a cigarette, his hand trembled.

Clifford sat on a divan, knees separated, head down, fingers playing with a paper napkin in his lap. He looked like an athlete worried about exams. Buckingham sat a cushion away from him on the divan, looking away, stroking his chin.

Arlington sat alone at the poker table, hands folded before him: a chief accountant awaiting the final tally. Oland sat, skinny bare legs crossed, in his usual chair, gazing into the fire.

Hands behind his back, his back to the room, Wahler stood in the dark far end of the room, studying the mounted head of a moose.

Dunn Roberts stood at the other side of the fireplace, near the arched service door, hands in his jacket pockets. Ashley, at the short side of the bar table, was making himself a drink.

"Thank you." Flynn dropped his tea bag into the cup of hot water Rutledge handed him and drowned it with a spoon. "Would someone please summon Taylor?"

"Coffee?" Rutledge asked Concannon. "Drink?"

"Coffee. Black."

Dunn Roberts pushed an ivory button in the wall.

"Seeing Taylor conspired with you, last time, to destroy evidence..." Flynn added.

When Rutledge handed Cocky the cup and saucer, Cocky took only the cup. Rutledge put the saucer back on the table.

Flynn wrung his tea bag out on the spoon and put the spoon with the tea bag in it into Cocky's saucer on the bar table.

Taylor came into the room through the little door behind Dunn Roberts. He was dressed in black trousers, his white serving jacket, white shirt and black tie. Flynn noticed that Taylor's eyes sought out Clifford's, but that Clifford did not look up.

Rutledge had made himself a weak drink.

Flynn took a chair some distance from the fire but facing it, at an angle.

Arlington said, "I suppose you want to know where we all were."

"I have no questions," said Flynn. "I've never been too keen at parlor games. Some people are better at them than others. Two men are dead. Murdered. You gentlemen are guilty of concealing a capital crime, destroying evidence, whatever. Most likely at least one of you is guilty of murder. This is not a civil situation. It's criminal."

Standing by the bar table, drink in hand, Rutledge simply gazed at Flynn.

Flynn placed his empty tea cup on the table beside him. "I have orders to give."

"We'll do whatever you say, Flynn," Rutledge said.

"Yes, you will. In this country, I hardly need to remind you, no one is above the law. I know there are others of you here, and among your membership, who represent law in its various aspects, but you summoned me here because I am not one of you. Detached." Sitting in the soft leather chair at midnight, warmth coming to him from the fire, Flynn remembered he had had very little sleep the night before. "Disinterested is the word. And as a disinterested representative of the law, I must not only tell you that what you did last night was wrong, it was criminal, imprudent for your own sake, and that tonight I must enforce upon you what is right."

Cocky was blinking in slow motion.

"Tell us what to do," Rutledge said.

Flynn hitched himself up in his chair. "We're calling the local police, your Chief Jensen, as a matter of courtesy. We are

108

also immediately going over his head and calling in the Homicide Squad of the State Police." Even to his own ears, Flynn was sounding detached, disinterested. "We are reporting the murder of Judge Robert Lauderdale. Until authorities arrive, everyone is staying in this room." Cocky was so relaxed, so near sleep, his empty coffee cup was tilting in his lap. "When Jensen gets here, I shall show him the murder room, making sure he disturbs nothing." Flynn's voice was becoming more and more distant to him, like a donkey engine he had started somewhere, and from which he had walked away. "When Jensen gets here..." The light in the room seemed to be lowering. The crackle from the fireplace was becoming louder. "When the State Police arrive..."

From the dark room, big white faces emerged.

Rutledge's was smiling.

With difficulty, Flynn turned his head to look at Cocky. Asleep. Cocky was asleep in his chair.

"Wahler..." Flynn said.

At the other end of the room, Wahler turned. Hands still behind his back, he, too was watching Flynn.

"Bastards," said Flynn. "You've all just been waiting...."

109

22

The fire was still going in the grate, but it seemed smaller, less bright, less important in the room. Grey daylight came through the small windows.

Cocky was still asleep in the chair. The coffee cup had been picked from his lap. Flynn's teacup and saucer were gone from the little table beside him.

All the glasses and cups which had been around the room the night before were gone.

Flynn looked at his watch. A quarter past nine. In the morning. Monday morning. The Rod and Gun Club. Lauderdale.

Standing up rapidly caused nausea to leap from Flynn's stomach to his head. He closed his eyes.

"Ach. It must have been a strong drug to put me to sleep, right in the middle of what I was saying!"

He took some deep breaths. Rubbed his temples with his finger tips. Waited a moment.

With heavy feet, muscles doing only a percentage of their job, he left the great hall, crossed the foyer, went down the corridor.

The door to the music room was open.

The daylight in the room, however gray and subdued, seemed unnatural to Flynn.

The room seemed natural enough. There was no corpse slumped over the piano. The piano bench was placed properly, invitingly empty. On the piano was Lauderdale's little music box.

Through the glass door Flynn saw the stretch of cold, yellow lawn, the flat gray lake.

He could not remember if, the night before when they found Lauderdale, the music box had been on the piano.

Back in the great hall he pressed the small ivory button in the wall. The clubhouse was deathly still.

He shook Cocky's left shoulder. Then, remembering, he shook Cocky's right shoulder.

Cocky's eyes opened, unfocused.

"Misery loves company," Flynn said. "Wake up."

Cocky looked around the room as if he'd never seen it before.

Flynn said, "They've absconded with what was Lauderdale."

Cocky pulled himself up in the chair somewhat sideways. He blinked.

"We've been had, my man," Flynn said. "Never mind. After you're awake a few minutes, you'll feel worse."

Taylor stepped through the small service door.

"Good morning," Flynn said.

"Good morning," Taylor mumbled.

"Were you part of the conspiracy to drug us?"

Taylor looked at his strong, uncalloused hand. "If they say I was."

"That's the way of it, is it?" Flynn's voice echoed inside his own head. His legs did not want to remain standing.

"Don't know what you mean."

"Where is everyone?"

"Gone hunting."

"Hunting?"

"Deer hunting. Left almost an hour ago."

Flynn's mind's eye saw the straggly line of well-dressed hunters, each carrying a rifle, walking into the woods together.

He shook his head. That hurt.

"They said they were going hunting this morning," Taylor said. "They went."

Leaning over in his chair, Cocky asked, "We were drugged?"

Flynn looked at the carpet. Its pattern was in sworls. Sickening sworls. "Where's Lauderdale?"

"He's been removed, sir."

"I know he's been removed! To where, damn it?" Flynn pressed his hand against his forehead. No answer was

111

forthcoming. "I know. You just work here. And a bloody good job you do, too. Body removals in the midnight!"

"Mister Rutledge said you'd have questions this morning, sir."

"Bright man, that Rutledge."

"He said I shouldn't try to answer them. That if you knew anything, you'd just try to contact the local police —"

"Brilliant man, that Rutledge."

". . . and just confuse things."

"Frank," Cocky said from his chair. "I don't feel well."

"Just don't think of pickles and creamed corn."

"He said you should hold your questions until you see him or some other member."

"Go get them," said Flynn.

"Can't. Don't know where they are."

"Bang the damned gong!"

"Wouldn't do any good," Taylor said. "It's not time for a gong. They'd just know it's you."

The thought of hearing the gong go off just now had less appeal to Flynn than pickles and creamed corn.

"They'll all be at Rumble de Dump at about twelve, shortly after."

"Rumble de Dump! That's a place?"

"It's a cabin, one of the cabins, up in the mountains. I'm bringing a hot lunch up to them. I'll be leaving in the Land Rover about eleven thirty. Why don't you come with me?"

Flynn's watch read nine-twenty-six. The last eleven minutes had passed like a full evening of Schönberg — interesting, but grating.

He had two hours to reglue his head and body for a ride doubtlessly over bumpy mountain roads in a Land Rover.

"Get us some breakfast," Flynn said.

"Oh, Frank."

"Breakfast has been cleared away," Taylor said. "When members miss breakfast —"

"We're not members!" Flynn exclaimed in the quietest shout he could manage. "We don't care spit for your rules! If the

112

kitchen staff are gone, you get us breakfast yourself. Scrambled eggs. Toast. Tea."

"Oh, Frank."

"Chicken soup."

"Chicken soup?"

"Chicken soup. If you have to lasso the chicken and pluck the feathers yourself."

"Yes, sir."

"Bring both breakfasts to my room in fifteen minutes."

"Yes, sir."

"Frank...."

"And bring me some walking boots. Size ten. A warm parka."

"Yes, sir."

Flynn swayed, just slightly. "And if you don't, Taylor, I personally will see to it that *The Wedding March* is played everywhere you go for the rest of your life, night and day."

23

After Flynn shaved, showered, hot, cold, hot, and dressed in fresh clothes, he felt confident enough to move his Bishop to King Knight Five.

At ten minutes to ten, Taylor was laying out breakfast for two in Flynn's room. There was a full serving bowl of chicken soup, as well as the eggs, toast and tea.

Cocky dragged through the open door. He, too, had shaved. His hair was wet. His eyes seemed somewhat brighter. His lips were still more slack than usual.

"At least," Flynn said, "I see little reason to interview Governor Caxton Wheeler and Walter March at this point." Shaking his head felt better this time. "Although I'm not even sure of that."

Cocky looked at the chessboard.

"Ah." Flynn rubbed his hands together. "What's better than chicken soup for breakfast?"

"Having no need for it."

Before closing the door, Taylor said, "I'll come get you, Inspector Flynn, about eleven thirty."

"You do that." Flynn drew a chair up to his breakfast. "Don't forget the coat and boots."

Cocky approached his breakfast as a kitten does a damp spot.

"We've been managed, Cocky. We've been outmanaged. I guess the characteristic of the managerial class is . . . that they can manage. That they must manage. Just as the working class must work."

Cocky watched Flynn ladle the chicken soup into Cocky's bowl. "I don't think I can stand a Jeep ride this morning, Frank. I had drinks with Hewitt last night, as well as whatever Rutledge slipped into my coffee."

"You stay here, Cocky. Try and re-assemble your brain. I'll go stalk the armed hunters in the woods." Flynn filled his own soup bowl. "I don't see what else we can do. We can't summon the State Police to see a corpse that isn't. Eat your soup."

Once Cocky brought himself to try the soup, he managed to consume a good quantity of it.

To encourage eating under these circumstances by distracting from it, Flynn kept up a chatter: "Taylor could be our man, you know. He's not one of this jolly band of preppies. Judge Lauderdale once sentenced him to three years in prison for octopusial bigamy. Then got him this monkish job here, as further punishment for his transgressions. Taunted him with his music box, if you'd believe it. Who'd ever think of a music box as a weapon?"

"So it was Taylor who hid the Judge's music box in the storage room?"

"Ach, your brain engine is turning over already. Eat some toast. I'd say that's a fair certainty. And, the music box was neatly on the piano this morning. Do you remember if it was last night?"

"A memorial. A victor's way of marking the spot of his victory."

"Is that what a memorial is? You may be right. Anyway, Taylor had a clear route. Up the cellar stairs from the gymnasium in bare feet, onto the veranda, through the music room door, a short leap to stand behind Lauderdale, those strong hands and arms neatly cutting Lauderdale's neck in half with a simple piece of clothesline, and quickly and quietly back to the gymnasium right under the music room. Both the bulkhead door and the door to the music room were open."

Cocky watched Flynn dispose of his soup bowl and serve himself some eggs. "Why would Taylor want to kill Huttenbach?"

"Envy, my lad. Envy. Taylor tells me he's been diagnosed by the prison psychiatrist, female, please note, as oversexed. Lieutenant Concannon, our lad Taylor had contracted himself to nine wives, if you believe it, nine, probably before he'd ever signed up for Social Security. That's why he works here: to keep himself from repeating those words more fatal to himself than all the rest of us, 'I do, I do.' Now Huttenbach, also an attractive young man, is known to be easy with the ladies, too. He attracts them easily, and conquers them easily. Wise enough to marry only once, though, although I'm not sure he displayed the greatest wisdom in marrying the hateful woman he did. If you were Taylor lying in your cold, celibate servant's cot under some wet eaves of this rustic edifice, hearing the jolly tales of Huttenbach's conquests while serving the boiled fish, wouldn't you be tempted to go blow his head off, too?"

"Yes," Cocky answered readily enough.

Flynn tried not to react to how readily Cocky answered that question.

"What about Clifford?" Cocky asked. "He's an attractive young guy, too. Why wouldn't Taylor envy him just as much?"

"Clifford's been away the last six months, in the Middle East. Taylor's only been here nine months. But the reasoning leads us to warn Clifford, doesn't it? Aren't you going to try the eggs?"

"Not sure I dare."

"Do." Flynn reached over and removed Cocky's soup bowl and spooned him out some eggs. "Think what some hens gave up for you: their posterity."

"It's my immediate future I'm worried about," Cocky said.

"Speaking of Clifford: Among the women the married Huttenbach shared the warmth of his loins with was Clifford's unmarried sister, Jenny. Insists it doesn't bother him, but there are brothers, and there are brothers."

"What would Clifford have against Lauderdale?"

"Don't know. He was a friend of Ashley, I presume, and a probable investor in Ashley-Comfort. By the way, I suspect that somehow Clifford has earned the displeasure of Buckingham. I saw a little incident through a window. Governor Buckingham is Clifford's uncle."

"Phew. This place is like a nest of worms." Having said that, Cocky averted his gaze from his eggs.

"Worms have nothing to do with eggs, Cocky. Dispel the thought of worms entirely from your mind. Eat your eggs. Don't give worms another thought."

Cocky lifted himself from his chair and limped over to the chessboard.

"Ashley seems our most likely candidate," Flynn continued. "Clifford says Huttenbach, without warning, dumped Ashley-Comfort stock at the worst possible moment for Ashley: reason for murder. In the reorganization of Ashley-Comfort being worked out in the back rooms of this den of equity, Lauderdale was trying, successfully, I suspect, to do Ashley out of the new company altogether: reason for murder."

"Wahler isn't one of them," Cocky said. "Not a member of the club."

"Who knows a great deal about everything, I suspect, the ins and outs of every relationship. He's one of the executors of Rutledge's considerable estate — a business empire, I gather. Who knows what game he could be playing?"

Cocky had moved something on the chessboard.

Coming back to face his breakfast again, he said, "D'Esopo isn't one of them, either. Not a member."

"Wouldn't that be something," Flynn said, having drained his first cup of tea. "Discover the Boston Police Commissioner a multiple murderer. Arrange Lauderdale's death in cahoots with Taylor, let's say. Another outsider. That would get you back on full pay quick enough, I don't think! Reminds me. Must see if Grover has checked into the kennel yet."

"Good morning, Grover. Glad to catch you in on a Monday morning."

Before putting through the phone call, Flynn had seen Cocky had moved his Queen to King.

Grover's response was a whirring noise.

"How goes the *affaire* Hiram Goldberg?"

"Took me hours."

"Sorry."

"Never got to bowl."

"Sorry."

"Well, it means I won't get my league shirt."

117

"Don't you have a shirt?"

"Not a league shirt, Inspector."

"Oh, I see."

"You know how the Commissioner is."

"Last seen sweaty and trembly."

"What?"

"Tell me how the Commissioner is."

"I mean, Commissioner D'Esopo."

"Oh, that Commissioner."

"I know you don't know him very well, Frank."

"Not well enough apparently."

"He avoids you the way every other real cop does. Professional police officer. He thinks you're as crazy as everyone else does. He's said so. He said so at that Labor Day picnic."

"I didn't attend."

"Course you didn't. We probably didn't even let you know there was a Labor Day picnic."

"Probably not."

"You're not one of us, Frank."

"Thank the Powers That Be."

"No one ever understands what you're saying. No one evem hears you, you talk so soft. When we do hear you, we don't understand you. Always making some kind of private jokes."

"Grover—"

"See what I mean? Always calling me Grover. My name is Richard Thomas Whelan. My friends call me Dick."

"That's rich."

"You didn't come up through the ranks, like the rest of us. The Commissioner wouldn't have anything to do with you."

"I wish he'd had less."

Grover paused. "Who's Les?"

"Grover, you're a very discouraging item to talk to on Monday morning."

"Anyhow, if you knew the Commissioner a little better, you'd know that nothing is more important to him than the fraternity of us police officers."

"Something is more important to him. At the moment."

"What? You just tell me what."

118

"Extricating himself from quicksand."

"What the hell are you talking about?" Grover sounded truly angry. "That's it, Inspector. Always saying things no one understands. Was that supposed to be funny?"

"You tell me about the Commissioner. Did you say your name is Dick?"

"He encourages things like the Police Bowling League. Says it helps build a sense of fraternity among us. He's even come out and bowled with us. You never have."

"The noise, Grover. Being in a bowling alley is like volunteering to conduct an orchestra of thunder storms."

"What! What are you talking about, Inspector? Conduct thunder storms!"

"You're right, Grover. One doesn't conduct thunder. One conducts lightning."

"Stop talking that way! God damn it! You're driving us all nuts, Inspector. I'm talking about the Commissioner, and you're talking about thunder and lightning storms!"

"They both exist in depressions."

"What?"

"Lows, Grover."

"Good-bye, Inspector."

"Wait, Grover. You need to tell me who knocked Hiram Goldberg off his two-wheeler."

Grover's sigh came from his toes. "I proceeded to 212 Fairview."

"Did you get there?"

"The home of Willard Matson, the man who owns the car reported stolen Saturday night, discovered within walking distance of his own apartment Sunday."

Grover awaited a rejoinder. Flynn said: "Yes?"

"Had to wait hours. The Matsons did not return to their apartment until after nine. About nine twenty. They were with their child in the hospital."

"What's wrong with their child?"

"I don't know."

"You didn't ask?"

"Inspector, what the hell has their child —"

119

"Find out."

Another heavy sigh. "I inspected the Matson car."

"Did Matson seem nervous?"

"Damage to the front right bumper and fender. Front right headlight was smashed."

"Go on."

"Matson said the damage must have occurred while the car was stolen."

"He admitted it was recent damage."

"He had to. We could ask neighbors —"

"Right. So did you have the car impounded?"

"It took me until one fifteen this morning, Inspector."

"Did you stay with the car all that while?"

"I stayed with the car or with Matson. I had to go inside, use their phone."

"I see."

"One fifteen."

"And forensic are examining it now?"

"Yes."

"No report yet?"

"What do you want, Frank? It's only eleven fifteen Monday morning. Where the hell are you, anyway?"

"Never mind. It's only eleven fifteen Monday morning. Did you find out if there was any way Matson and Goldberg could have known each other?"

"I did find out that Matson is a school teacher. Teaches seventh grade at the local public school."

"Some discovery. You asked him what he does for a living."

"He's black."

"A black school teacher. A Jewish jeweler. I suppose they could have met at a meeting of The Daughters of the American Rebellion."

"I don't think they knew each other."

"When will forensics have its report ready?"

"They didn't say."

"You didn't ask."

"I have a question for you."

"Ach," said Flynn. "Finally a spark of interest in your work."

"I need to know the answer."

"Finally conducting an investigation, are you?"

"I'm doing a survey. How do you feel about creamwitches?"

"What?"

"Creamwitches. You know, those thin, little ice cream sandwiches. The machines which dispense them are very expensive, but if enough officers —"

"Good-bye, Grover."

"Inspector, Commissioner D'Esopo thinks the work the Eats Committee is doing is damned important, and if you won't cooperate —"

"Call you later, Grover." Flynn hung up.

He chose an apple from the bag Cocky had brought him the night before and went over to the chessboard. "What-what," he muttered. "Grover says 'what' and I say 'what.' Grover and I talking to each other is almost as bad as an Englishman talking to himself. What?"

He moved his Queen to Knight Three.

Immediately, Cocky moved his Queen Knight to Queen Two.

"I see you've been thinking about this."

Taylor knocked on the door and entered. Over his arm he had a lined hunting jacket and in his hand a pair of thick boots.

"Ready, sir?"

"Am I ready to ride over the mountain and confront a band of miscreants, at least one of whom is a murderer, all of whom are armed?" He moved his Queen Knight to Queen Two. "Yes, I'm ready."

24

"Did you sleep well?" Rutledge sat on a rock over a fire outside the small, square log cabin called the Rumble de Dump.

"I've slept better, thanks," Flynn said, strolling to him. "And with less encouragement."

"I bet you want some coffee." A steaming mug was in Rutledge's hand. A coffee pot was on a stone at the edge of the fire.

"Not from your hands, I don't."

Rutledge laughed. "No hard feeling, I hope?"

"Why not?"

Clearly Rutledge disdained someone who did not accept apology. "Sit down, Flynn. Trust me that much."

Flynn sat on a rock lower than Rutledge's, but still away from the fire's smoke.

His head and stomach had taken better than expected the long jouncy ride over the hills to the Rumble de Dump. Still, he felt somewhat unfocused and wobbly in the knees.

On the long ride, Taylor had spoken only twice. After a stretch of washboard road, he said: "Driving this thing always makes me want to pee." As they approached the cabin, he said, "Near the Rumble de Dump, up on a little bluff, there's a great view." Flynn had not answered.

As soon as they arrived, Taylor opened the back of the Land Rover. Individual, covered metal dishes were being kept warm in an electric oven at the back of the Land Rover.

Then Taylor had gone into the woods.

No one else was in the clearing at the front of the cabin. Obviously, Rutledge had been expecting Flynn, was waiting for him.

One rifle was propped against the cabin's outer wall, near the stone step to the front door.

"I trust you understand the spirit in which we did what we did," Rutledge said.

"Oh, aye," said Flynn. "A bunch of overaged schoolboys

scurrying around a big old place at midnight, playing another trick on authority, removing a corpse, destroying evidence. A marvelous lark."

"You had seen the body. You had seen what evidence there was."

"Have you ever heard of forensics?"

"Enough to know it doesn't count for as much in a capital trial as people like to believe."

Flynn sighed. The man had an answer for everything. "What did you do with Lauderdale? Try to make it seem he strangled himself in all those telephone wires at Timberbreak Lodge?"

"One of our members has a horse farm about a hundred kilometers from here. Lauderdale was visiting him this weekend, you see. He went out yesterday on a horse by himself and didn't come back. The horse returned last night. His body was discovered this morning."

"In an evening gown?"

"That's the point, Flynn. You think we're going to permit the police and press in to see Judge Robert Lauderdale strangled to death while wearing an evening gown? The man deserves better than that. He was a distinguished justice."

"Justice."

"He remarried last month."

"He did?"

"In fact, he married Ernest Clifford's mother."

"He did?"

"Sort of an elopement. All very romantic."

"Is that why Clifford came back to this country?"

"Not for the wedding. I said it was a kind of middle-aged elopement. They honeymooned in Palm Desert."

Against the dark bark of the trees ringing the cabin, Flynn could see a few snow flakes falling.

"Lauderdale, despite his proclivity to dress in drag and make us all laugh, was a normal male in every other respect. He has three children by a previous marriage."

"I didn't see that he made you all laugh."

123

"He did. We were all pretty used to his antics. But he was funny."

The Rumble de Dump was about halfway up a small mountain. The ring of trees immediately outside its clearing sheltered it and deprived it of a view.

"How does one get strangled falling off a horse?" Flynn asked. "Tell me that one."

"His neck was broken. We took advantage of that. Thanks to you, we didn't make the mistake we made with Huttenbach the night before. As Wahler said, we should have shot him again, from closer up, to make the suggestion of suicide more real."

"Glad to have been of such help," Flynn said sourly. "You damaged Lauderdale's neck enough so that no one could see he had been strangled?"

"The horse stomped on it. Other parts of his body as well. Sure you won't have some coffee?"

"You had the horse stomp Lauderdale until a hoof happened to land on Lauderdale's neck?"

"That's about it."

"And you had changed him from an evening gown to some riding clothes."

"That's it." Rutledge poured himself more coffee.

"You're a cold-blooded bunch."

"We did what we could do for Lauderdale."

"And for yourselves. Preserving the flamin' privacy of your club. Continue to conceal who-knows-who through The Rod and Gun Club."

"We have a right to protect our privacy, Flynn."

"You're a clique."

"Right," said Rutledge. "Just like your local Parent-Teachers Organization, P-2, or the Russian Politburo. The decisions we make are apt to be in our own best interests. Does anyone think differently?"

"You're making decisions for the world at large without any input from the world at large."

"We're making decisions for ourselves, and implementing them in the most efficient way possible. Tell me who doesn't."

"I wasn't so drugged, Rutledge, that when I entered the music room last night, having come from just next door, that I forget that I found you standing over Lauderdale's corpse."

"I was in the corridor, coming from the communications room, when I heard Lauderdale's strange noises. I heard the groan, in his own voice. I looked in. He was slumped over the piano."

"I wouldn't be surprised if you were managing this whole thing. Huttenbach's murder, getting me here, Lauderdale's murder..."

"I expect to be under suspicion. I expect all of us to be under suspicion. Except Arlington."

"Why not Arlington?"

"In all the years I've known him, I've never known Arlington to kill a fish or shoot an animal, not even a bird. He just comes out with us on a day like this and prowls around the woods by himself. I'm sure if he ever saw a deer close up, he'd try to pet it."

It was a light, fine snow. Flynn heard the flakes landing on the dry leaves.

"Rutledge, why do you want me here?"

Rutledge drank from his cup. "To investigate. D'Esopo says you're a genius. To find out who killed Huttenbach, and now Lauderdale. We want to know."

"I'm not sure that's a true answer."

"Why else?"

"Maybe you just want a headmaster figure to play with, someone to enjoy getting around. So you can have someone to put asleep in his chair while you tiptoe around playing your midnight tricks."

Rutledge stood up and emptied his coffee cup onto the ground. "I drink too much coffee."

"I'd hate to see you get all nervous."

From down in the woods came the sound of a voice calling.

"Again, I assure you, Flynn, we did nothing last night, after knocking you and your friend out, without consultation with some of the most respected names in this country."

"Preserve us..."

In the woods below them a man was shouting loudly.

"Preserve us our institutions," said Rutledge.

"Hey, someone!" the voice in the woods shouted. "Anyone! Come here! Quick!"

Flynn stood up.

There was a quick volley of six rifle shots from down the mountainside.

Flynn and Rutledge ran in the direction of the shots.

25

"**I** fired the shots," Clifford said. "I wasn't sure anyone could hear me yelling."

Face down on the dead leaves, feet separated, arms flung out, was someone who'd had the back of his head bloodied by a hard blow. Snow was jeweling his rough jacket. His orange hat was a half meter from his head, upside down near the base of a big tree. Near it, at a curious angle, was a hunting rifle.

And not far from the body was a stout, solid tree branch about the size of a baseball bat: a perfect weapon.

"Who is it?" Flynn asked.

"Ashley," Rutledge said at his shoulder.

"He's dead," Clifford said. "I'm pretty sure he's dead."

Flynn crouched over Ashley and felt for a pulse. There was none.

When he looked up he saw Buckingham tearing through the woods toward them. Arlington was picking his way downhill more precisely. Taylor was running straight downhill from a different angle. Dunn Roberts puffed up behind Flynn.

"Ashley, Ashley, Ashley . . ." They sounded like choirboys whispering the name of the next hymn to be sung.

In his steady pace, Hewitt came straight uphill and stopped just outside the group. There was no expression in his brown eyes as he saw the corpse. The hunting guide was used to seeing bloodied creatures fallen on dead leaves.

D'Esopo, dull-eyed, lumbered in from around the big tree. He, too, was used to seeing bloodied, fallen creatures.

Wahler stayed on a path as he came through the woods. His trousers were a red corduroy; his coat calfskin. He wore a scarf.

A man Flynn did not recognize immediately joined the peering faces. Wendell Oland, dressed. His hunting clothes looked too big for him. He looked different in clothes: older, and yet more childish somehow.

Everyone was carrying a rifle except Rutledge and Taylor. Flynn was surrounded by eight rifles pointing at the ground.

And everyone had come from a separate direction.

"Ashley, Ashley..."

"I was just coming up for lunch," Clifford said. "I damned near tripped over him."

"Did you hear anything, see anything as you approached?" Flynn asked.

"His hat. I wondered who had lost his hat."

Flynn looked up into Rutledge's eyes. "He could have been dead more than an hour."

Rutledge continued to look at the corpse.

All but Hewitt and Arlington wore leather gloves. Hewitt's and Arlington's were wool. Taylor's hands were in his jacket pockets. He had not worn gloves on the drive up to Rumble de Dump.

All but Clifford, Arlington and Oland held their rifles in walking positions in the crooks of their right arms. Arlington's and Oland's were in their left. Clifford held his in both hands across his blue-jeaned thighs.

There was no immediate way of telling whether the back of Ashley's head had been struck from the left or the right. He had been clubbed hard, straight on.

Flynn stood up. He stepped over Ashley. Being careful not to disturb Ashley's hat, he stood with his back against the thick tree.

"How are you going to manage this one?" he asked. The circle of men looked from Flynn to the corpse back to Flynn again. Clifford wiped his nose with his glove. Only Hewitt looked away. Managing was not in Hewitt's line. "I'm sure you're already trying to figure out something..."

"I don't blame Flynn," snapped Arlington. "Certain decisions have been made around here, and the situation has gotten worse rather than better. It looks to me like this whole affair had been mismanaged."

Mismanaged, mismanaged. The phrase had a boardroom ring to it. Call the office of the manager, and speak to his secretary, mis-managed.

"Right," chimed in Clifford. "Maybe if we had done something different when Dwight was killed . . ."

Buckingham, Rutledge and Roberts seemed more complained against than complaining. And Wahler seemed to be a spectator. Beside Flynn, D'Esopo remained dull-eyed. Hewitt just stared at the corpse. Taylor's eyes were as lively as ever. The man's ebullience was irrepressible. Flynn saw Taylor catch a snow flake on his tongue.

"I was with Oland," Arlington said. "All morning. I can say that much."

"You were not!" exclaimed Oland.

Arlington flushed.

"I was alone all morning," Oland said, "No one was with me. I didn't hear a shot, either."

"He wasn't shot," Clifford said.

"What do we do now?" Roberts asked.

"I'd like Mister Wahler to go back to the clubhouse with Taylor and call the police," Flynn said. With the oven in the back of the Land Rover there was room left for only the driver and one passenger. "It may seem a radical suggestion to you gentlemen, but this is the third murder in a row, and I think it's time the authorities were notified. Of course, the last time I made that suggestion, I was knocked unconscious for hours while you scurried about altering evidence. Let me warn you — "

"Why Wahler?" Rutledge asked abruptly.

"He's a member of the bar," said Flynn; "not a member of the club."

"Rutledge should make the call," Arlington said.

"Why not Flynn?" asked Buckingham.

"I'll call, if you like," said Flynn. "As long as you understand I shall do nothing to put a good face on all your crimes and misdemeanors. Should any of you still be in doubt, let me assure you, gentlemen, your power and prestige don't impress me much. Even if I don't make the initial telephone call, I expect to give evidence, fully and truthfully, as would any other good citizen."

"You're supposed to help us," Oland said petulantly. "Who's doing these murders?"

129

"I don't know," Flynn said. "Doubt I'd tell you if I did know."

"Why not?" Buckingham asked.

"Not sure what you'd do with the information if you had it. Or what you'd do with the culprit if you had him. You haven't given me much reason to trust you. I hate to think of the extents to which you gentlemen might go in behalf of efficient management."

"Flynn, I think you're overstepping—" Rutledge began hotly.

"I'd make a citizen's arrest of you all now," Flynn continued in his mild voice, "if such had any real meaning in a snowy wood. Instead, I'm going to ask you all to tiptoe away, leaving the evidence around Ashley's murder undisturbed. Go back to the clubhouse. Wahler should go with Taylor in the Land Rover and call the authorities. By the time the rest of you gentlemen have walked back to the clubhouse, at least the local police in the person of Chief Jensen should have arrived. The State Police should not be far behind. I'll take a look around here, if you don't mind. I intend to be a good witness."

The men stood silently a moment, looking back and forth at each other. Clearly their instincts wanted a board meeting, with the advice of bought expert consultants. None wanting individual responsibility for this positive step, they wanted a shared irresponsible consensus against it.

"He's asking us to turn ourselves in," said ex-Governor Buckingham.

"To the Chief of Roads," Clifford giggled.

"You haven't much choice," Flynn said. "You've had three murders in thirty six hours. Who's next, Governor, you? You, Clifford? How about you, Rutledge? Wahler?" Flynn shifted his back against the tree. "Sorry, boys. There comes a time when things get out of hand. Members of the grown-up world have to intervene."

"You're not one for rules," D'Esopo said. Then he cleared his throat.

Flynn looked at him in surprise. "What are you saying,

130

Eddy? That we let this situation continue? Find Oland dead at six o'clock, Arlington at ten?"

"It's a matter of police work." D'Esopo began moving away from Flynn, around the outside of the circle of men. "You can do better than the local guys. You can do better than this."

He trudged up the hill toward the Rumble de Dump.

"We'll do as you say," Rutledge finally said.

He nodded to Taylor and Wahler and led them up the hill behind D'Esopo.

Silently, the other members wandered away, taking slightly divergent routes back to the main clubhouse. Arlington walked behind Oland.

"Want me to stay here?" Clifford asked.

"I do not," Flynn said. "But you might tell me what you're still doing here at The Rod and Gun Club. Why haven't you flown up the chimney by now?"

"What do you mean?" the big young man asked.

"Didn't I hear that your new stepfather fell off a horse last night? Had his neck broken and crushed? Why haven't you rushed to console your mother, his new bride?"

"Oh." Clifford looked at Flynn from under heavy brows. "Uncle Buck said we were not to leave, either of us, until you had come up with some answers. Anyway, my mother's buried two husbands. And Lauderdale had his own kids. . . ."

Hewitt had cleared the wet leaves away from the base of another tree and sat down. His back was against the tree; his rifle over his knees. He looked ready to remain there until the spring thaw.

Flynn asked Clifford, "How did you like the idea of Lauderdale being your stepfather?"

"Things aren't that way, Flynn. With Jenny. Or my mother."

"What way?"

"What they do with their lives is strictly their own business."

"You mean you don't care about your mother or your sister?"

131

"That's not what I mean. . . ." Clifford's eyes moved over the ground almost as if he were looking for a place to be sick. He did not say what he did mean.

"The prince came home on his charger," Flynn said, "to make all right at the castle. Is that it?"

Clifford was staring at Ashley on the ground. "Honest, Flynn. I thought Ashley was the murderer. The guy was getting desperate, maybe going nuts. . . ."

Flynn, too, looked down at the corpse. "Honestly," he repeated. "So did I. What's more, I'm still not sure he wasn't."

Flynn turned Ashley's body part way over from both sides, enough to examine cursorily the man's front.

Hewitt watched him from the base of the tree.

Then, on hands and knees, Flynn combed through the leaves on the ground in a wide area around the body. No calling card turned up, not that any, at that point, would have done much good. Each of the suspects had been in that area.

He was combing very close to the body when he heard someone coming down the hill. He sat back on his heels and looked up.

Wahler. Still carrying his rifle.

"What are you doing here?" Flynn asked.

"Thought I'd come tell you," Wahler said, standing over Flynn. "Rutledge went back in the Jeep with Taylor."

"Posh-tosh," said Flynn. "Rushed back to make new arrangements, I dare say."

"You're not going to get these men to turn themselves in," Wahler said. "They each have too much to lose. Together, they have everything to lose."

Flynn said, "It must have been the effect of the drug. I was having a drug-dream."

Heavily, he stood up. He brushed the knees of his trousers.

To Hewitt, he said, "You'll stay here? I'll send the police out to you as soon as I can."

Hewitt nodded.

132

"And how long will it take us to walk back to the clubhouse?" Flynn asked Wahler.

"More than a couple of hours."

With a gloved hand, Flynn picked up the tree branch he believed had been used to club Ashley to death. "Just what I need: to spend a snowy afternoon walking through the mountains."

26

With Wahler, Flynn entered the Rod and Gun clubhouse through the front door. None of the members was about.

"Don't tell me we got back before them," Wahler said.

Going up the stairs in their wet boots, they passed a Vietnamese coming down in slippers.

In his room, Flynn put the tree branch across the top of his bureau and took off his coat.

On the bed was the Monday edition of the local newspaper. On the front page was a story of Huttenbach's death. A story. Flynn scanned it as he sat on the edge of his bed taking off his boots.

> While staying at Timberbreak Lodge, Bellingham, United States Representative Dwight Huttenbach was killed Saturday night when his shotgun discharged accidentally while the Congressman was cleaning it . . .
>
> Boston Police Inspector F.X. Flynn, who happened to be staying at Timberbreak Lodge over the weekend, reviewed the findings of Bellingham Chief of Police Alfred Jensen . . .

"And neither confirmed nor denied," Flynn muttered to himself. "Sometimes silence is dross."

Cocky came through the open door. "Wahler said you had to walk back."

"You leave this here for me?" Flynn waved toward the newspaper.

"Yes."

"Complicity." Flynn stood up in stockinged feet. "I am guilty of the complicity of silence." He studied the chessboard. Cocky had moved his King to Rook One. "I don't suppose there's tea water bubbling on that bar table downstairs?"

"There isn't. Just booze. I guess they don't put out the coffee and tea service until after dinner."

"Ashley is dead. Did Wahler tell you?"

"No."

"Smacked on the back of the head, I suspect with that tree branch." Flynn moved his King Rook to King One. "Everyone assembled over the corpse, from different directions, mind you. I gave a long and tiresome speech — a continuation of the speech I was giving last night when we both fell asleep — insisting the authorities be called in, and notifying them I intend to be a good witness. Then Rutledge grabbed the Jeep and came back here, I presume, to telephone fellow members around the world, to figure out how best to obstruct authority now. You haven't seen Police Chief Jensen around, have you?"

"No."

"Any chunky lads identifying themselves as representatives of the State Police?"

"No."

"I got outmanaged again. When did the other members get back?"

"I haven't seen anyone. I didn't hear them come back."

"How do you feel?" Flynn asked.

"Okay. I got a couple of hours sleep."

"Nothing like a mountain walk in the snow to clear the head," Flynn said.

"Frank, doesn't one more murder help clarify things?"

"Indeed," said Flynn. "Ashley may have had reason to kill Huttenbach and Lauderdale. He may even have done so. He may have had reason to kill himself. He did not do so. If one is up to doing oneself in by clubbing oneself in the back of the head, then one has extraordinary reason to continue to live: a good job with the circus."

"Yeah," Cocky said. "Win an Olympic gold medal for gymnastics."

"I told Rutledge Ashley could have been dead more than an hour, because Rutledge had spent the previous half hour talking to me. He could have killed Ashley and been waiting at the cabin for me when I arrived. But the temperature was below freezing; the ground was cold. Ashley could easily have been killed after we arrived."

135

"We,'" repeated Cocky. "You and Taylor."

"Yes. Immediately after we arrived, Taylor disappeared into the woods. To relieve himself, he said. To see the view, he said. On a cloudy day, mind you, just before it began to snow. No one is eliminated. Clifford found the body. By the by, ol' Cocky, Rutledge tells me Lauderdale married Clifford's mother last month, eloped with her, during Clifford's absence abroad. What do you make of that?"

Cocky's eyes had wandered to the windows. "It's snowing pretty hard. Is it accumulating?"

"Not that much. I left Hewitt with the body. So: Everything is becoming about as clear as the weather."

"I found something interesting," Cocky said. "A huge vault. There was one locked door in the communications room. I opened it. Behind it is a man-sized vault door. Winchell, *circa* 1958."

"You opened the locked door?"

"Yes."

"But you didn't open the vault?"

"Thought I'd better have your permission."

"You mean, my complicity. Do you think you can open the vault?"

"Sure. I learned how when I was on the Burglary Squad. It's an old, simple kind of safe. Child's play."

Flynn gave Cocky a long look. "My, my. If only Commissioner D'Esopo knew of all your talents, Cocky, you'd be back on full pay fast enough. You could help him break into the refrigerator after hours."

"Shall we go open the vault now?"

"No." Flynn sat on the bed again, near the. pillows. "No more complicity for me. It is well past time to summon the local authorities. I believe it a fair assumption that the playful members of The Rod and Gun Club again have avoided turning themselves in. I am about to do so." He picked up the telephone receiver.

The telephone was dead in his ear.

"Oh, my," Flynn said after waiting a moment for an

136

operator to answer. "They've done this, too. Cut off the phones. Cocky, please go to your room and try that phone."

Flynn listened to the silence coming from the telephone. He might as well have been holding a shoe to his ear.

Cocky limped back into the room.

"Nothing?"

"Nothing."

Flynn put the phone back in its cradle and reached for his boots. "Get your coat, Cocky. We're going for a ride."

27

"I think the car that was there was a Cadillac."

"Whose?"

"I don't know."

In the short walk from the clubhouse to the car park, Cocky had begun to shiver. Flynn realized that Cocky was outdoors seldom nowadays. He had become acclimated to the overheated police building on Craigie Lane.

"What's the make of the car that left and came back?" Flynn asked.

"A Mercedes."

In the five or six centimeters of snow that had fallen, tire tracks made it perfectly clear that some time ago two cars had left, probably at the same time. One car had returned, very recently. The tracks went down the slope, around the lake toward the main gate.

"This old beauty has a marvelous heater," Flynn assured Cocky as he started the engine of the ancient Country Squire station wagon. He fiddled with the dashboard knobs. The wipers cleared the windshield of snow. Cold air blasted their faces and knees. "In a moment you'll feel as warm as a politician being audited by the Internal Revenue Service."

"I wonder who left," Cocky said into his coat collar. "Who came back."

Flynn backed the car around. In the snowing dusk he turned on his headlights. He followed the tracks down the slope and around the lake.

"Frank?" Cocky asked. "Do the great variety of murder weapons puzzle you?"

"Indeed they do."

"A shotgun," mused Cocky. "A piece of rope. A club."

"Different methods of operating altogether," agreed Flynn.

"That usually means different people are doing the murders."

"It could mean that," said Flynn. "Or it could mean one person taking whatever opportunities present themselves."

"Are half the members of The Rod and Gun Club killing the other half?"

"What for?" asked Flynn. "Some traditions are better not started."

The car slipped a little going around a curve in the woods.

"Obviously they're not all of the same political party. Dunn Roberts — "

"Ach, no, it's not that. People who play with power so stratospherically support all parties. They cover their bets. They don't care so much who is in power, so long as they have influence. And they make sure they do."

"Then what issue would divide them?"

"To the point of wholesale murder? I don't know. Maybe somebody's grandfather insulted somebody's grandmother. Maybe somebody put frogs in somebody's bed at school a million years ago."

"Maybe it's a kitchen revolution. We've paid little attention to the kitchen help."

"A Vietnamese was in the front of the house when Wahler and I came back from our walk. He was coming down the stairs as we were going up."

"Somebody has to make the beds, I guess." With the fingers of his right hand, Cocky turned the heater down. They were now being blasted with equatorial air.

"I keep thinking of blackmail." Flynn slowed as they approached the fence. "The situation is rife for blackmail. All these important men runnin' around dressed anyway at all, or no way at all, drinkin', gamblin', shootin', and swearin', havin' these meetings they think aren't being overheard..." A few meters from the gate he stopped the car. "But for the life of me, I don't see how blackmail ends up with three men murdered."

"By different methods."

"By different methods, yes."

The gate was closed, of course. The tire tracks travelled under it and continued into the woods beyond.

Flynn blew his car horn.

139

No guard appeared.

No light shone from the windows of the guard's hut. No smoke came from the chimney.

"Are we captivated?" asked Flynn.

He blew the car horn again. No guard appeared from any direction.

"No one's here," Cocky said.

"You might as well stay here." Flynn got out of the car.

He walked forward in the headlights of the car. His shadow was enormous against the fence, on the snow beyond.

Behind him, the car door closed.

There were three stout chains locking the gate, one at head height, one at waist height, one at knee height.

"I could pick the locks," Cocky said from behind Flynn, "if we could reach them."

Flynn reached for one of the chains with his gloved hand, to try pulling the padlock nearer, tight against the other side of the fence.

Something chopped the back of his neck.

He found himself sitting in the snow, his right leg under his left knee.

Cocky's right hand was gripping Flynn's elbow.

"Electrified," Cocky said. "The fence is electrified."

"Shockin'," agreed Flynn. He shook his head.

Cocky kept his hand on Flynn's arm until he regained his feet. Then Cocky stood back and studied the gate.

"Ramming it with the car. . ." Cocky said.

". . .would make an awful mess. And get us nowhere. I think such is called an accident. You'd need a tank. . ."

Cocky considered the whole fence. "Can't go through it or over it."

"We're prisoners," admitted Flynn. "Should have guessed it when the phones didn't work."

Cocky was shivering again.

"Let's get back in the car," Flynn said. "As long as we're now prisoners of The Rod and Gun Club, there's something else I want to check out."

140

As they approached the clubhouse, Flynn turned the car lights off. There was enough light in the snow for him to see their way.

Beyond the clubhouse, he turned onto the forest road he had travelled that morning with Taylor.

Just after he turned on the headlights again, the car hit a snow drift. Flynn swung the wheel and the car straightened itself.

"Do you think we dare chance it?" Flynn asked. "I'm headed for the Rumble de Dump."

"Sure. Why not? Might as well freeze to death in a snow drift as be shot, strangled or bludgeoned."

"A positive point of view."

"They say people freezing to death hear celestial music."

"Oh? Do you get to pick your own tune?"

"What music would you choose?"

"Something by Tchaikovsky, I expect. Warms the blood."

"You're a practical man, Frank."

The car skidded going up a hill. Flynn raised his foot from the accelerator and it straightened out.

"Evidence being destroyed almost as soon as it is created by our murderer or murderers..." began Flynn.

"Surely not murderess."

"...I find myself excusing my usual comfortable method of detection."

"Which is?"

"Seeking the controlling intelligence. The one mind controlling the current situation, capable of doing these murders, destroying the evidence, etcetera, regardless of apparent motive, apparent opportunity."

He pumped the brake going downhill.

"Which is?"

"Rutledge."

The rear end of the car swerved into a drainage ditch. Its own momentum bounced it out again.

"Frank."

"Yes, Cocky."

"It isn't that I don't want to hear your theories."

"Oh?"

"All very interesting."

"Thank you."

"Enlightening."

"Good of you to say so."

"And, I'm sure with a very few more logical steps, will lead us to the right conclusion."

"Your faith in me is edifyin'."

"But, at the moment, I'd rather have you concentrate on your driving."

"I thought you were driving."

"No, Frank. You're driving."

"I see."

"I'm not all that fond of Tchaikovsky myself."

"Prokofiev?"

"I'd rather hear the children singing carols a month from now."

"Are you sure? Think of what you're sayin', man."

"I'm sure."

"Sleigh bells ring; are you listening? All that again?"

"Furthermore," Cocky concluded, "in my humble opinion, Wahler controls Rutledge."

The trip to the Rumble de Dump took more than twice the time it had taken that morning.

Flynn turned the station wagon around in front of the cabin before getting out. He left the engine running.

"You might as well stay here," he said to Cocky through the open door. "You've only got street shoes."

Cocky stayed in the car.

Flynn walked through the clearing in front of the cabin, into the woods where he and Rutledge had rushed that morning at the sound of shouts and shots. Steadying himself with the odd birch sapling, he slipped and slithered down the steep hillside.

"Hewitt?" he called.

Except for the crinkling of the landing snow, the woods were silent.

With more snow, the woods looked different.

Flynn was certain he had found the place where Ashley had been killed. His body had lain face down under that tree. Hewitt had settled down under that other tree. That is where the tree branch used as a club had been.

Except Ashley's body wasn't there.

Neither was Hewitt.

In the fresh snow there was no evidence either had ever been there.

There was no evidence anything unusual had ever happened there.

Overhead, a tree branch cracked cold.

The snow was wetting Flynn's face.

"So." Flynn knew talking to the trees was exactly as good as had been his talking to the men assembled under these trees a few hours before. "Hewitt is in on this, too."

28

"Who's missing?"

Cocky and Flynn stood in the doorway of the great hall of The Rod and Gun Club.

The fire was roaring. Naked, except for a book on his lap, Wendell Oland nodded asleep in his usual chair by the fire. Around the poker table in boisterous play were the once-and-future Governor Edward Buckingham in a tattered old bathrobe, Senator Dunn Roberts in a sweat jacket, smoking a cigar, Boston Police Commissioner Eddy D'Esopo, in black shoes, also smoking a cigar, Ernest Clifford, his pile of chips looking huge against his dark blue sweat shirt, and banker Philip Arlington, despite his glasses, peering myopically at the cards on the table. In his white jacket, Taylor was filling the beer glasses on the table from a pitcher. Dressed in full shirt and necktie, Paul Wahler sat under a reading light away from the poker table, absorbed in a large book entitled *Contemporary Estate Planning*.

Clifford, Buckingham, Roberts and Taylor each glanced at Cocky and Flynn in the doorway. None offered any sort of greeting.

"Rutledge," Flynn answered. "Rutledge is missing."

"But I thought you said Rutledge's car is a Rolls Royce — not a Cadillac."

"Wahler drove me to Timberbreak in the Rolls. I assumed it was Rutledge's. Let's go see."

Upstairs they went to the end of the corridor. Flynn knocked on the door of Suite 23.

No answer.

Flynn knocked again, louder.

Still no answer.

He tried the door handle. The door was unlocked.

Flynn pushed the door open with his fingertips.

A hunting knife, inserted at an upward angle from the base of Rutledge's rib cage, pinned him to the big blossoms of his chair.

144

His eyes were closed. His hands were folded neatly in his lap.

The front of his woolen hunting shirt, his hands, his lap were thick with blood.

"Why do they need to keep us?" Flynn asked testily. "It seems the process of elimination is working perfectly well all by itself."

He touched the blood in Rutledge's lap with the tips of his fingers. "Not too warm."

The reading lamp on the table beside Rutledge was lit.

Putting his glove back on, using only his index finger and thumb, Flynn picked up the telephone receiver by its mouthpiece and held it near his ear. The line was dead.

Also on the table was a note pad. Leaning over it, not touching it, Flynn read:

Arlington —
in capitol — too much
Buckingham/frame
2) Brigadoon 100

"Can you make out if that's an *o* or an *a* in *capitol?*" Flynn asked, moving aside.

After looking, Cocky said, "I can't be sure."

"I make it out an *o*."

Looking around the room generally, Flynn said, "He was attacked from the front."

"By someone he knew."

"Of course."

"The handle of that knife should give us some nice fingerprints."

"If you notice, Cocky, we're both carrying gloves."

"So, probably, was the murderer."

"Someone entering this room, wearing or carrying gloves, when it's snowing out, would not have caused either alarm or suspicion on Rutledge's part."

"I suppose if the murderer thought there might be fingerprints, he would have taken the knife with him."

"He's done nothing wrong so far — unless you consider the antisocial aspects of the murders themselves." Flynn snapped on

145

the light in the bedroom of the suite. Everything was orderly. It looked as if the room had just been cleaned. Turning back to Cocky, he said, "And, you notice, another method of murder: stabbing."

"Frank, you said you saw a member of the kitchen staff coming down the stairs when you were going up."

"Yes." The gong sounded. Flynn looked at his watch. "Our playful polar bears now repair to the sauna, I guess."

"Should we stop them? Do the who, where, when and why immediately?"

"No." Flynn turned off the light in the bedroom. "Let's take this opportunity, while we know where everyone supposedly is, to put you and your curiosity to work in that vault."

Flynn took a long look at Rutledge.

Even stabbed to death in his chair, Rutledge did not look surprised.

Cocky went first through the door to the corridor.

Flynn took the key from the inside of the lock, closed the door, and locked it.

"As corpses seem so hard to keep track of around here," Flynn said, "let's try to keep this one to ourselves."

29

"Millions!"

"It's not millions."

Flynn didn't dare peer through the small round window of the sauna. He could not do so without being seen by the men inside.

He stood in the gymnasium out of sight of the windows, trying to ascertain who was in the sauna by identifying the voices.

"Bless my pointy Irish ears," he said to himself.

"Too damned much money. And I don't see it's doing us any damned good." That was Buckingham's slightly whiskey-grated voice.

"The arrangement was made." Arlington's voice was precise, pedantic.

"Yeah, but this was not why the arrangement was made." Dunn Roberts' was the reasonable voice of a committeeman.

"The arrangement was made—"

"To keep you whole, financially, while you're jerking the strings of the federal government." Buckingham.

"Okay. Everyone agrees having Arlington an economic guru in Washington is of benefit to the club and everyone in it." Clifford's voice was clear, young, virile.

"Should be." And Oland's was soft, old and somewhat petulant.

"And is it proving a benefit?" Wahler's voice had both deference in it and the prosecutor's edge.

"Of course." Arlington.

"No. I really mean, are there benefits which can be simply evidenced on paper to support the belief that Arlington's being in Washington—"

" 'Evidenced on paper!' I hope not!" Buckingham.

"You may be sure, my being in Washington has been of enormous benefit to The Rod and Gun Club and its members."

"There's no reason why Arlington should suffer financially by government service. Especially when he has friends." Oland.

"He had to separate himself from his banking income —" Clifford.

"Overtly, yes." Roberts.

"His personal expenses rose. His personal income diminished." Clifford.

"So he was given access to The Rod and Gun Club's capital." Oland.

"It wasn't our point to permit him to greatly increase his personal wealth." Buckingham.

"Why wasn't it? It can be assumed that, during these years of his private life, he would be doing so, if he were in the private sector." Oland.

"Not to the point of grabbing capital, making personal investments with it, taking the profits himself." Buckingham.

"I'm not sure you're right." Oland.

"What good does it do the membership?" Roberts.

"A certain amount of tit for tat. The point is that the membership benefits in other ways. I have no doubt that it does." Oland.

"The point, Oland, is that a hell of a lot of capital has been appropriated by our friend, Arlington." Buckingham.

"And if we all get killed off. . ." Roberts.

"Don't be ridiculous." Arlington.

"Tell me who approves of what you're doing. Not Rutledge. Not Lauderdale. Huttenbach wanted a complete accounting, immediately." Buckingham.

"It was Ashley who blew the whistle on you, Arlington." Clifford.

"A personal accounting? How dare any of you —" Arlington.

"It seems we need something, Arlington." Clifford.

"What I'd like to know is what is the consensus now about Ashley-Comfort? Now that Ashley's dead." Arlington.

"I guess there are no obstacles to our doing what we want now." Roberts.

"Arlington, you're changing the topic of discussion. You've put your hands on millions . . ."

As Buckingham continued the indictment in the sauna, Flynn drew quietly away.

Arlington, Buckingham, Clifford, Roberts, Wahler, Oland: They were all baking in the sauna, while Cocky was breaking into the vault.

"Good man." Flynn stood in the door of the vault.

Under a single, dangling light bulb, file folders at his feet, Cocky stood inside the vault.

The vault was as large as a walk-in closet. Deep filing cabinets stood tight against each other from floor to ceiling. There wasn't really room for Flynn to enter.

"Everyone's accounted for," said Flynn. "They're chirruping away in the sauna like so many broilers singing *Home on the Range*. Except our honored Commissioner of Police. If he's in the sauna with the rest, he is maintaining a humble silence."

From an opened drawer, Cocky took another folder and dropped it on the pile on the floor.

"By the was, it was an *a*. I refer to the cryptic note on Rutledge's telephone pad. Arlington is too much into the *capital* of The Rod and Gun Club. The complaint is not that he is spending too much time in the *capitol*. In fact, if I interpret correctly the chirruping I just heard from the chick incubator, I'd say that the membership of The Rod and Gun Club essentially provided Arlington with the means to feather his own nest while in Washington, in return for federal favors generally done the membership. But Arlington seems to have taken a bit too much advantage of the offer, and certain members began to cry 'Foul!,' among them, Ashley, Huttenbach, Lauderdale, and Rutledge. Now Buckingham, in particular, has begun to peck away. And, sure, wasn't it Rutledge who said Arlington was incapable of violence, that if Arlington '*ever saw a deer close up, he'd try to pet it*'?"

"For all his economics degrees, financial wisdom, position

in the banking world, Arlington himself isn't all that wealthy."

"Beginning to discover things already, are you?"

"His father lost the family fortune and went deep into debt trying to build a railroad along the Amazon River."

"The Amazon," clucked Flynn, "has taken in much more gold than it has ever given up. So the present-day Arlington had every reason to discover how money works on paper."

"But he's never really had any of his own."

"If I understand what I just heard, Arlington recently has appropriated barrels of the stuff. And, of course, being draped in the federal mantle, he knows they won't publicly call him to account. Ach, well, I'm sure it's all a game the boyos are playing to squeeze ever more favors out of the current federal economic guru. What else are you finding, Cocky?"

"The behind-the scenes story of American political, business and family life for the last century, is all."

"What? All in this wee room?"

"Damn' near, Frank. Personal notes and comments written in dozens of different hands regarding anybody who was or is anybody."

"My, my. How does it work? Who actually keeps the records?"

"I guess they keep it on each other. Explains the dozens of different kinds of handwriting, over the years. I guess when one of them knows something significant about another, he makes a note of it, and it ends up in here."

"And why wouldn't the maligned party come in and take the note about himself out, expunge the record, as it were?"

"I don't know. It must be against the rules, I guess."

"Schoolboy honor," said Flynn. "One doesn't look in the school records regarding oneself. Intrinsic faith in the social system. Enough to make you sick, Cocky."

"Listen to this." Cocky knelt on the floor of the vault and with his right hand flicked open a folder. "This is just the first folder I happened to grab. I studied it to see how the file-keeping system works. It refers to a man who was a member of Teddy Roosevelt's cabinet.

His sister, Mary, known to keep to the farm in
New Hope, commonly thought to suffer tuberculosis,
is reported by her maid (who came to us on The Main
Line) as syphilitic. It is fair to suppose she has such
from her late husband, who was known to sow his wild
oats in New Orleans. However, the possibility cannot
be ignored that she has it from her father, about whose
early life in France little is known. If she does have
it from her father, the present cabinet member must
be closely watched for any symptoms of this mentally
debilitating disease."

"Posh-tosh," said Flynn. "The dear lady might simply have
preferred the company of cows to people."

"The file goes on, of course. Fifteen years later, in a
different handwriting altogether, there's this note:

Charles, the Ambassador's nephew, applying
to us generally for recommendation to Harvard, has
been advised instead to think of a career on the
family's ranches in Montana. The family is thought
to have a history of syphilitic madness, as Charles'
mother, Mary, died at the farm in New Hope
without having been seen by anybody in
ages."

"That will teach you not to snub society! Pull on your
corsets and go out to the party, or your blood will be ostracized
for generations to come!"

"Would you believe it, Frank? All on the gossip of a maid!"

"What's the most recent entry in the folder?"

Cocky turned over the bulk of papers to the last.

Mary, at the age of twenty-one, has taken her
Ph.D. degree in astrophysics from Cambridge
University, England. She has accepted a position at
Smithsonian Observatory, Harvard.

151

"Ach! The family might be becoming useful again!"

"But there's nothing more about her. And the note seems years old."

"She's a female."

Cocky stood up and returned to the file drawers. "I'm just digging out the files regarding the Arlingtons, the Buckinghams, the Cliffords, so on."

"Don't be too long in what you're doing. I have difficulty believing, no matter how strong the pull of tradition, that our jolly hosts will actually run naked from sauna to freezing lake in a snow.storm."

"You mean, you're not joining them?"

"Under the circumstances, a warm nap in my room seems the more healthful exercise. I'll swing the vault door almost shut, so the outside door can be closed."

"Don't lock me in here."

"And why not? I can't think of a greater luxury than a warm room, a good light, and a century of fascinatin' readin'!"

•

30

Flynn's telephone rang.

He looked at it incredulously.

He had just entered his room.

He grabbed up the receiver. "Thank you for calling."

From the other end of the telephone connection came difficult breathing, the wet sound of blubbering, and what was most likely a woman's voice saying something about "Inspector Flynn."

"Elsbeth?" Flynn asked the phone. "Is that you?"

Not Elsbeth. Flynn had never heard his wife blubber but was pretty sure, if she took to blubbering, her blubbering would not sound like this.

"Operator? Don't hang up."

"It's real urgent. Inspector Frank Flynn."

"Whoever you are, don't hang up. Is this one of the operators? One of the operators at Timberbreak Lodge?"

"Inspector Flynn?"

"Yes, this is Flynn. Don't hang up."

"Thank God! You've got to help us."

"I'll do anything I can. Just don't hang up."

"They've come and taken Willy away. In handcuffs!"

"Willy. I'm sorry to hear it. Who's Willy?"

"My husband. Is this Frank Flynn?"

"Yes, this is Frank Flynn. Inspector. Who are you, please?"

"Stacey Matson. I know your wife, Elsbeth. We're on the Mayor's Special Committee to Build Intra-District After-School Sports. Elsbeth Flynn."

True: Flynn's wife, Elsbeth, served on a committee to build intra-district after-school sports programs for teenagers. Also true: The committee had been named by the Mayor. Flynn was never sure how special that made it.

"Stacey Matson?"

"She's a good woman, your wife."

"Thank you, I say for her."

"A few times we've had coffee together, after the committee has met, you know? She's had me laughing about her life, the hard times, in Israel, and even earlier, and how you two met, always a refugee, she says of herself."

Elsbeth could make anyone laugh. Clearly this woman, Stacey Matson, was not laughing now. She was barely able to control her crying to speak.

"Yes?" Flynn encouraged. "You know my wife?"

"Willy is a good teacher, Mister Flynn. He's about the best there is. You can ask anyone, any of the other teachers at the school, the kids... He's turned down an executive..."

Willy Matson. Teacher.

"Ach!," said Flynn. "You're the wife of Willard Matson. Of something-or-other Fairview Road."

"Two-twelve."

"Hiram Goldberg."

The name set off a wave of hysterical weeping from the other end of the telephone connection. Flynn waited for the woman to regain control of herself.

"Billy..."

"Take it easy, Mrs. Matson. Whatever you do, don't hang up. Has your husband been arrested for the hit-and-run killing of Hiram Goldberg?"

"They arrested him. In handcuffs!"

"Your car —"

"Billy! It was Billy!"

"Someone else was driving the car?"

"Billy went through a plate-glass window on our sunporch. He was running in the house and tripped, skidded on this little throw rug... His head...through the window..." Stacey Matson sobbed. "Bleeding. His neck was bleeding, his shoulder, arm..."

"Is Billy your child?"

"He's in the hospital. Loss of blood."

"How old is he, Mrs. Matson?"

"Six. Six years old. Willard was meeting with the people down at the church. Montague had picked him up."

"Mrs. Matson —"

154

"Willy's told the police he was driving the car. He was at church."

"Okay, I —"

"I was driving the car. Billy was on the front seat, on the blanket I grabbed up. More and more blood. I was driving to the hospital. Billy to the hospital."

Flynn's mind's eye saw the scene easily, horribly. A woman, a mother, frantic, hysterical, partially blinded by tears, driving her profusely bleeding child to the hospital, driving because she had no alternative but to drive him herself, looking at her child on the car seat beside her soaking a blanket with blood, coming to an intersection after dark, not seeing an old man pedalling a bicycle slowly, just getting through traffic, getting through an intersection, getting her bleeding child to the hospital, perhaps not even knowing she hit an old man, ran over him . . .

At The Rod and Gun Club the gong sounded. Immediately the spotlights outside went on. The swirling, furious snow outside Flynn's window came alive in the light.

"It was the bleeding from his neck . . . how long did he have to live? I don't remember . . . hitting anybody. I don't know. I never saw a bicycle . . ."

"I'm sure you didn't see the bicycle," Flynn said softly.

Through his window, Flynn watched the naked men dash through the calf-high snow and plunge into the lake. Clifford, Buckingham, Arlington, Wahler tonight, even old Oland, Roberts: all who were left.

"Willy has told the police he was driving. He was at the church, Mister Flynn. I wish he'd been home. I was driving. I had to get Billy to the hospital quickly. I never hit anybody. But I must have. They said the car —"

"Who made the arrest?" Flynn asked. "Who arrested your husband?"

"The police. Some sergeant came last night when we got home from the hospital he was here looking at the car came back this afternoon —"

"Please, Mrs. Matson, for your own sake, try to collect yourself. Take some deep breaths while I talk to you. Will you do that?"

155

"...All right. Elsbeth always said you're some kind of...
reluctant, she said."

"Just listen a minute". Flynn spoke slowly, softly, calmly.
"The law really isn't a bad guy. It's not really there just to create
misery for everybody. You can trust the law to have some
understanding. Your car may have hit Goldberg. Probably did.
After you hit the bicyclist, you didn't stop. Here there are clearly
what are called extentuating circumstances. You did know you
hit something or someone because your husband drove the car a
mile from your house and reported it stolen."

"He said, 'What happened to the car?' You know, when we
came out of the hospital. Saturday night. I said, 'Oh, God,
Willard.' Then I remembered I hit something. A noise. A bump
in the road. We ran over something. Only then did I remember.
Willy said, 'If you don't know what happened...'" Mrs. Matson
again choked with tears.

"You can expect some understanding from the law, Mrs.
Matson. Mrs. Goldberg has lost her husband —"

From the other end of the telephone connection came a true
wail.

"Come on, woman. Pull yourself together. Mrs. Goldberg
is a human being, too. Maybe a mother. Her old husband was
out pedaling a bicycle after dark. Trust people to have some
sense."

"The police sergeant who was here —"

"Never mind what he said. These things take time. The law
moves slowly, Mrs. Matson. There'll be plenty of time for
everything to get said, everything to get understood."

"I was trying to tell the sergeant I was driving, I...I was
crying so hard."

"Pulling yourself together is now your job. Is there someone
who can stay with you?"

"My sister's here with me now."

"Good. How's Billy doing in the hospital?"

"They're finding more blood for him. He almost died. The
stitches —"

"See? Things are looking brighter all ready. I'll be back in
Boston sooner or later," Flynn said, almost adding *If at all.* "And

156

then, believe me, you'll have the full benefits of my, ah, reluctance. In the meantime, it is most important you do me a favor . . ."

Sniffling was abating. "A favor?"

"Yes. I seem to be stuck at a phone through which I cannot make outgoing calls. Do you understand?"

A sniffle.

"But your incoming call got through to me. Therefore, it is most important that you call my assistant and get him to telephone me at this number." Flynn gave her the telephone number complete with area code and even gave her his room number. "Have you written that down?"

"Yes."

"The man you are to call is Sergeant Gr— Richard T. Whelan, Dick Whelan—"

"Sergeant Whelan? That's the same man who arrested—"

"Yes, yes. This is a case where you just have to separate bananas and apples, Mrs. Matson. It's terribly important that you tell Sergeant Whelan to call me at this number immediately. He's to keep calling until he reaches me. You'll do that?"

"Yes."

"If you don't connect with Sergeant Whelan immediately, tell anyone on the Boston Police you speak to, to contact me immediately at this number."

"I understand."

"By the way, how did you get this number yourself?"

"I called Elsbeth, Elsbeth Flynn's number. Your son answered. He heard me crying. He told me to call you directly. He gave me this number."

That Winny. So efficient.

"Right. After talking with Sergeant Whelan, will you call my wife—"

"They're gone."

"Gone?"

"I never spoke with Elsbeth. Your son said she was outside, waiting for a van. They've gone to a concert in Worcester."

"Ach, they'll be gone until midnight." Flynn then said: "It's a school night!"

157

"I'll try the number for you, but I'm sure they're gone."

"Yes, do. Then try to get some rest."

"They have Willy in jail!" Fresh tears bubbled through the phone line.

"They're not hurting him, Mrs. Matson. They're just booking him. Did either of you ask for a lawyer?"

Outside, with greater haste, the men were rushing through the snow up from the lake. Waving his arms, walking backward, Arlington clearly was trying to hurry Oland along.

"We don't have a lawyer."

"Don't be afraid of anything. It will take a judge to set bail. By that time, maybe I'll be back. . . ."

"Thank you, Flynn. Inspector."

"Try not to worry. Your son will be all right. Your husband's all right."

"Oh, I pray the Lord."

"Get some rest. But please call Sergeant Whelan first."

"I will, Inspector. Thank you."

Holding the receiver in one hand, Flynn broke the telephonic connection with the fingers of his other hand. Putting the receiver back to his ear, he released the button.

The line was dead.

He dialed O.

The line remained dead.

Outside, the spotlights went off.

Flynn put the telephone receiver back in its cradle.

There was a gentle knock on his door.

Softly, Flynn said, "Come in, Commissioner."

31

E ntering Flynn's room, Police Commissioner Eddy D'Esopo said, "Been looking for you."

Flynn came around the bed. "Oh, I've been taking a stroll through the woods, as did yourself. Then I went for a bit of a sleigh ride."

D'Esopo looked large and dark and heavy in the small room. Both his size and his boyish grin doubtlessly had contributed to his rise to the top job in the police force.

"You skipped the sauna and cold bathe?" Flynn asked.

"I took a short cut: a warm shower in my room."

Flynn's borrowed hunting coat was on the bed. The tree branch that might have been the weapon that killed Ashley was on the bureau.

"Frank, we need to talk."

Flynn sat in his chair at the chessboard. "Pull up a pew."

D'Esopo sat heavily on the bed, on the other side of the coat. "I owe you apologies. For whatever damned fool thing I said to you out in the woods. For getting you up here in the first place, getting you into all this . . ."

"You made a mistake, all right," growled Flynn. He leaned over to take off his hiking boots. "You had too much faith in my amazing intellect. You thought I'd arrive in the middle of the night and reveal all with the rising sun."

"Not really. Your intellect does amaze me. At least, I hardly ever know what you're talking about."

"Maybe because I'm very stupid."

"And you know more about this kind of people . . . Well, I mean, Frank, you didn't work your way up threatening pushcart peddlers with citations in the North End."

"You really don't know much about me, Eddy." Flynn pushed his boots away with his stockinged foot.

"I've guessed a few things, over the years. Frank, since you came on the Boston cops you know I've been asked not to pry into your background. And you know what? I may be wrong, but it seems to me this request has come from the same sort of people who are the members of The Rod and Gun Club. Am I wrong? A call from The White House switchboard, a letter from a Supreme Court Justice, cryptic letters from this agency, that agency. Washington, Ottawa, London. What am I supposed to think?"

"What, indeed."

"Then you come here and disdain these guys, insult them. I'm not blaming you."

"Oh."

"You can understand my calling you up here in the first place. And then you brought Concannon."

"You are blaming me for that."

"By the way, where is Concannon?"

"Looking into something for me."

"Originally, it was just Huttenbach who was dead. The members ran around, adjusting the evidence — "

"I never knew you were so given to euphemisms, Eddy."

"I knew you could work all that out." D'Esopo's hands seemed enormous on his thighs. "Yes, I did."

From his jacket pockets Flynn fished his pipe, tobacco, scraper, wooden matches and began to build himself a smoke. "And then Lauderdale, and Ashley, and . . ."

"I was not in on your being drugged, Frank. I just thought poor little Concannon fell asleep. When you began to turn vague and glassy-eyed . . ."

"And when the evidence regarding Lauderdale's death began to be 'adjusted,' as you put it? The corpse dressed for a horseback ride — "

"I had nothing to do with that, Frank. I went to my room."

"You went to your room, Commissioner, and let it happen."

"Listen, Frank, I've been honest with you. I'm indebted to these guys, more than I can ever repay."

"Is that what's bothering you?"

"What do you mean?"

"Ashley introduced you to this fun-and-games social club. Ashley's dead. Huttenbach's family foundation took on your

160

unwell child. Huttenbach's dead. What did Lauderdale ever do for you, Eddy, that you arranged his death?"

D'Esopo's eyes became huge as he stared at Flynn. "You're kidding."

Flynn was packing his pipe. "I think when most people think of murder, they think of it with a specific weapon in mind, either a gun, or a knife, or a club, or a rope. A policeman, such as yourself, Eddy, has the experience to think of murder as something that can be done in a variety of ways. You wouldn't expect someone with a policeman's experience to be consistent, necessarily, in the way he chooses to murder people. You've seen murder done by shooting, strangling, stabbing, clubbing...haven't you?"

The size of D'Esopo's eyes had not diminished. "Yes. Of course."

Flynn held the lit match over the bowl of his pipe and puffed several times. "Is that all you have to say?"

"Frank, are you out of your damned mind?"

"Always a possibility, of course." The pipe was going well. "How come you didn't react when I just included 'knife' and 'stabbing' among methods of murder?"

"Christ, I don't know what you're talking about. I never know what you're talking about."

For a short moment, Flynn wondered precisely how intelligent one has to be to become commissioner of police in a major city. Or how good an actor one must be.

D'Esopo put himself into a more relaxed position on the bed. He turned, leaned back and rested on one elbow. He looked less comfortable. "What I don't understand, Frank, is that although I think you know these guys better than I do, are more comfortable with them, you seem much more critical of them than I am."

"That's because I do know them."

"Okay, they're very upper class. I'm not one of them. As you pointed out, I never will be."

"The difference between us, Eddy, is that you won't be and I wouldn't be."

"What are you talking about? A bunch of guys who like to go hunting and fishing and play poker together — "

161

"They've bought you, Eddy. To the point where you summoned me up here to protect their privacy, or secrecy, if you will. They neutralized you, at least to the point that since Saturday night you have not functioned as a trained and responsible police officer or, even, frankly, a very good citizen."

"I said I'm indebted."

"You're also intimidated."

"That may be right."

"You have the idea that whatever these 'big guys,' in your view, do, must be right."

"I didn't become Police Commissioner without a certain amount of political savvy." D'Esopo stood up as if he were going somewhere and then stood still. He put his hands in his pockets.

"I'm sure of it," Flynn said.

"And if you're not a realist —"

"It's ever wrong."

"What's wrong? Make sense, God damn it, Frank!"

"Elitism."

D'Esopo's eyes were blazing down at Flynn in his chair. "If you know how to get along in this world without people, Frank, without a little 'you scratch my back, I'll scratch your back,' please tell me how."

"Sure, we all have places in our backs we can't reach," Flynn admitted. "Isn't that why we get married?" Flynn sucked on his pipe.

"Cut the bullshit, Frank. A few facts. I want to hear a few facts."

"Pick up the phone, Eddy." The Commissioner looked across the bed at the telephone. "It's dead. It's been cut off. You may not make an outgoing call. Try to leave the grounds of The Rod and Gun Club. The guard at the gate is gone. The gate is triple-chained and 'padlocked. And I can tell you from personal experience, the fence is electrified to a high voltage."

"Not true. This can't be true."

"What do you think of a system, Eddy, which neutralizes you, and me, and once we are neutered, to change a verb on you, keeps us prisoner?"

162

"Is this literally true, Frank? Or are you talking in some kind of high-nonsense symbols again?"

"Try the phone. We're prisoners, Eddy."

D'Esopo walked around the bed and picked up the telephone receiver.

Flynn glanced at his watch. Grover had not called in. No one from the Boston Police had. Had Mrs. Matson been too distraught to understand, to keep a promise? If one call had come through, another ought to be able to; or was that one call some sort of an electronic coincidence?

D'Esopo dialed *0*, waited another moment, rattled the buttons. Then, slowly, he hung up.

"I came here, to your room . . ." he said.

"Yes?" encouraged Flynn.

Not turning around, talking toward the wall, D'Esopo said, "I thought you might get further with your investigation if you cut the bullshit, had a higher degree of acceptance of The Rod and Gun Club, its members. . . ."

"At the moment, you're sounding rather lame, Eddy. They want to control the world. You. Me. They want everything their way. It's rather childish, don't you think? And, surely you'll agree, any society which serves boiled fish, broccoli and tapioca pudding as dinner ought not have control of the world."

D'Esopo turned, faced Flynn. "Frank, you don't seriously have me on your list of suspects. I called you up here."

"The list is getting shorter, Eddy. By the hour."

The gong sounded throughout the house and Flynn's head.

"Drinks," D'Esopo said. "That's the bell for drinks. I want a drink. What do I say to these guys?"

The door to the corridor opened.

His old police satchel under his right arm, Cocky entered.

"Ah, Detective Lieutenant Walter Concannon," Flynn said. "Retired."

"Hello, Cocky," D'Esopo muttered. "Frank, are you coming downstairs with me?"

"Not now." Flynn sat up in his chair. "The retired Detective Lieutenant and I are in the middle of an interesting chess game."

163

Flynn studied the board. "At least on the chessboard, Commissioner, we still have some freedom of movement."

32

"Sorry I took so long." After the Commissioner left Flynn's room, Cocky sat at his side of the chessboard, satchel at his feet. "Fascinating reading."

He moved his Queen to Rook Four.

"Good thing you didn't get caught."

"Yeah. Once I realized everyone must be back in the house, I snuck upstairs and got my satchel to transport the files. I came through the kitchen. The only one who saw me, besides the kitchen help, was Hewitt, getting kerosene for his cabin. Dinner, you may be relieved to know, is roast turkey."

"It's pretty hard to ruin a turkey, isn't it?"

"I'm sure they're trying."

Flynn moved his Bishop to Knight Three. "Either our boss, the esteemed police commissioner, does not know that Rutledge is dead, or he is willing to permit this particular employee to think he is indeed obtuse. I listed the murder weapons used so far as gun, rope, club and knife, and the methods of murder as shooting, strangling, clubbing and stabbing, mixing up the orders a little bit, I admit. And would you believe the Commissioner failed to ask me who has been stabbed with a knife?"

"Dumb like a fox." Cocky moved Pawn to Queen Knight Three.

"Obtuse as an ocelot." Flynn moved his Knight to Bishop One.

"Are ocelots obtuse?"

"Never met one, that I remember. I have met foxes, however. Upon meeting, I can't say I was ever favorably impressed by their intellectual capacities. Very few have been up to even lying convincingly about having read Proust. It's always been my impression, in fact, that those who pursue foxes have so little reason to flatter themselves that they assign an unwarranted degree of prowess to those they hunt. Just as I'm sure the ordinary house cat, among his own society, lauds the intelligence of the mouse unduly."

Cocky's Bishop took Flynn's.

Flynn's Rook took Cocky's Bishop.

Cocky said: "Dwight Huttenbach's granduncle, you'll be interested to know, entertained fourteen-year-old girls at tea every Sunday at his Fifth Avenue mansion. Speaking of cats and mice, that is."

"How did he entertain them?"

"Had them dress in tutus."

"How very entertaining for them."

Cocky moved his Knight to Bishop Four. "Dunn Roberts's great-grandfather bragged of having sired twenty-six illegitimate children."

"Some chaps haven't much to brag about, have they?" Flynn moved his Queen to Rook Three. "How many did he mention in his will?"

"Four." Cocky's Bishop went to Knight Two.

"They had good mothers." Flynn placed his Knight on Knight Three.

"And Lauderdale's mother originally was a member of the Washington Opera Company." Cocky moved his Queen to Rook Three. "A soprano. That doesn't surprise you, does it?"

"Sure, aren't we all satires of our parents?" Flynn moved his Bishop to Bishop Two.

"The most significant thing I've discovered so far is that Arlington was institutionalized, quietly, for a while. At a private psychiatric sanitarium, conveniently out of the country. British Columbia."

"That is significant. When?"

"Six years ago." Cocky moved his Knight from Bishop Four to King Five. "He had electric shock therapy."

"No wonder he's merciful to other beasts. Or so Rutledge testified, just before he was unmercifully skewered." Flynn's Queen went to King Seven.

"Frank, it indicates his personality has suffered a period of instability."

"Or someone thought so."

166

"He has had cosmetic surgery on his face," said Cocky shifting his Queen Rook to King One.

"Self-esteem. Extra need for self-esteem. Ambition." Flynn's Queen took the Bishop Pawn. "At the moment, he seems an impossibly tight, precise man. At poker, he almost gets the ink from the playing cards on the tip of his nose."

"And he's a top dog in the federal government." Cocky's Knight took Flynn's King Bishop Pawn.

"And his friends in The Rod and Gun Club, no matter how petulantly they complain in the sauna, in fact can leash him in any time they want." Flynn's King Rook moved to King. "But are you sure the story of his having been institutionalized is true? As you pointed out earlier, the membership is apt to place credence on the world of possibly vengeful housemaids."

"In the file there is what appears to be a detailed bill from the sanitarium marked 'Paid in full.'"

"That smacks of evidence." The gong sounded for dinner. Flynn even felt the sound through his stockinged feet on the floor. "They must have finished ruining the turkey. Have you discovered anything interesting regarding the relationship between Clifford and Buckingham?"

Cocky moved his Knight from Bishop Seven to King Five. "Buckingham is the brother of Clifford's natural mother."

"Who is now Lauderdale's widow." Flynn took Cocky's Bishop with his Queen. "Nothing else?"

"Nothing yet. Uncle Buck seems to run the family finances. If not run them, at least be principal financial advisor. I'll read more after I win this game."

"I wonder if any member of the club has succeeded in becoming his own grandpaw."

Cocky's Knight moved to Queen Seven. "Frank? Do you think anything could be going on between Clifford and Taylor?"

"You mean, anything sexual?"

"That's what I mean."

"Do you worry that they're both young and good looking?"

"Clifford's never married."

"A wise choice for a young journalist, I should think. Or, at

167

least, I've often heard old journalists say so." Flynn shifted his Queen Rook to Queen One. "And *not marrying* is not a charge one can ever level against young Taylor. He has demonstrated his liking for women by marrying not once but nine times."

"His liking for weddings, at least."

"I suppose if you're oversexed, as he says he is and, to some extent, has demonstrated, ultimately anything would seem more attractive than those infernal exercise machines."

"I'm just trying to think along the lines of more than one person doing these murders, some extraordinary relationship everyone has been overlooking. . ."

A knock on Flynn's door caused Flynn to say, "Maybe this is the help you need to win this game."

"Maybe it's some one, or all of them, come to murder us."

"Cocky, you shouldn't be that afraid of losing. . .Come in."

Dunn Roberts opened the door. He stood in the doorway looking from Flynn to the chessboard, to Cocky and back to the chessboard. "The dinner gong has sounded." With a finger he stirred the ice in his drink. "You missed having drinks with us."

"The last drink we had in your company," Flynn drawled, "was a little too strong for our tastes."

"Sorry about that."

Cocky said, "We have to eat, Frank."

"You go ahead down, Cocky." Pretending to reach across the board to Cocky's King Row, Flynn dropped the key to Rutledge's room in Cocky's lap. "Check, mate."

The right side of Cocky's face broke into a marvelous grin. "Really, Frank. You don't mind making any pun, do you?"

33

"Yes?" Flynn asked.

"Yes, what?" Senator Dunn Roberts said.

Leaving, Cocky had left the door to the corridor open.

"I suspect you want to say something to me."

"Wanted to make sure you guys come down to dinner. Can't have starving guests."

"Corpses is corpses." Flynn slid his shoes out from under his bed and started to put them on.

"I do have something to say." Roberts stirred his drink with his finger and then sucked his finger. "Apologies."

"Oh?" Flynn mocked surprise.

"We haven't made your job any easier, I guess. Putting knockout drops in your tea . . ."

"Senator, I have a job in Boston. Solving a hit-and-run killing. Testifying in court on another matter day after tomorrow. I never contracted for a job here at The Rod and Gun Club: I wouldn't expect payment or favors from you boyos if I were cut and bleeding on the sidewalk. Granted, there is a job for police who have proper jurisdiction. And I am not a part of the conspiracy to make sure that job does not get done."

Roberts sipped his drink. "You're not investigating?"

"I am being held prisoner at The Rod and Gun Club. Can't make a phone call." Shoes tied, Flynn was sitting back in his chair. He looked at the telephone near the bed. What happened to Mrs. Matson? She wasn't really that hysterical. Why hasn't Grover called? "We can't get through your gate, or around your electrified fence. Don't you know that prisoners do not make the most enthusiastic workers?"

Roberts' face flushed. He looked into his drink.

"All this is a terrible mess," he agreed quietly. "I've known Lauderdale all my life. Huttenbach's father called me the hour Dwight was born. Ashley and I won a tennis tournament together, at Exeter, when we were teenagers."

"And Rutledge?"

Roberts paused. "Rutledge really hasn't been any worse than the rest of us all through this. He's just more of a desk man, if you know what I mean. The decisions he was implementing were made by all of us and . . ."

". . . certain unknown people whose advice you all had by telephone."

"Yes."

"What did you do with Ashley's body?"

"Oh." Roberts looked into his glass again. Was he watching the ice melt? "Ashley had a car accident this afternoon. About fifty kilometers from here. Over the state border. Slippery road . . ."

"Was his car a Cadillac?"

"Yes."

"Who drove the Mercedes?"

Roberts shrugged. "One of us."

"So you put Ashley in his own car, and one of you drove him to the scene of his skidding accident, followed by another of you driving the Mercedes. After the accident was phonied up, the Mercedes picked up the driver of the then-smashed Cadillac and drove him back here."

"Yes."

"Then you all sat in the sauna together, discussed business, ran through the snow into a freezing lake, had drinks together and now dinner. Is that it?"

"Yes. I guess so."

"And will you sing at dinner tonight? Bang your beer mugs and chant *Rumble de dump* nonsense?"

Roberts shifted his feet. "Not tonight."

"Tell funny stories?"

"Okay. Think us a bunch of bastards. Traditions have been in motion here a long time — "

"And again you've guaranteed that the public, which is deeply affected by the decisions made here, still don't know that The Rod and Gun Club exists, that a certain judge knows a certain governor whose nephew is a certain journalist who knows a certain newspaper tycoon who knows a potential presidential candidate, all of whom are indebted to each other

170

for one thing or another, all of whom are seeing to it that a certain economic advisor to the federal government ends up his stay in Washington a privately wealthy man."

Watching Flynn, Roberts' eyes had narrowed. "I see you have been doing some investigating."

"When one sees a large, gray animal with four feet, floppy ears, a tail at one end and a trunk at the other, one is apt to call it an elephant."

Roberts waved his glass. "Come down to dinner. We all need to talk to you."

"To listen to me?"

Roberts smiled. "We might even listen."

171

34

"Having a twinge in my arm," Wendell Oland complained to Flynn. Naked at the table, the old man was exercising his left arm as well as space allowed. "Must have stressed it swimming, or something."

"Perhaps a little lineament?" suggested Flynn.

"Perhaps."

When Dunn Roberts led Flynn into the dining room, those who were left were seated in their usual places. Oland was to Flynn's left; Wahler to his right. To the left of Oland was Roberts's place. To his left, Rutledge's place was set, but empty. Lauderdale's place between Wahler and D'Esopo was empty, as was Ashley's place between D'Esopo and Buckingham. When Flynn sat down, Cocky nodded affirmatively directly across the table at him: He had checked — Rutledge's corpse was still locked in Suite 23. Arlington and then Clifford were at Cocky's right.

Flynn said to the table: "Senator Roberts says there is something you want to talk to me about."

"One or two things," said Clifford. "One or two."

"Isn't it pretty obvious?" asked Arlington.

"Only one thing is obvious to me," said Flynn. "What's obvious is that you gentlemen have given me no choice but to let you people continue killing each other off."

"All these people being shot," said Oland. "Who'd think Rutledge..." His voice trailed off as he paid attention to his arm.

Taylor and a Vietnamese waiter were bringing around the soup cauldron.

Everyone waited uselessly for Oland to finish.

"Where is Rutledge?" Buckingham asked.

"Must be working in his room," Wahler said. "Has to review some figures. He's talking to Tokyo later tonight."

"He must have heard the gong," Arlington said.

Flynn said, "Sure, that gong is enough to wake the dead, isn't it just?"

Oland turned in his chair and ladled the soup into his bowl himself, using his right arm.

"I'm sure he'll be right down," said Wahler.

Across the table, Cocky was watching Flynn, as if waiting for him to speak regarding where Rutledge was. Flynn said nothing.

Buckingham hitched forward in his chair. "I think it's time we put a few cards on the table."

"Your deal, Uncle Buck."

Leek soup was ladled into Flynn's bowl.

"I admit I didn't like Lauderdale," Buckingham said. "Never did. And I admit I wasn't too pleased when I got the wire from my sister saying she'd eloped with the son of a bitch."

"I think he would have preferred just 'bitch,'" Roberts said.

A chuckle went around the table.

"I didn't particularly like Ashley, either. And I admit I poured a goodly amount of capital into Ashley-Comfort recently, when that jerk Huttenbach pulled out, without a word to any of us. Ashley wasn't the wisest administrator. Huttenbach himself, in my opinion, was a charmless dolt. Life was dealing him much more than he deserved, and he never had the grace to realize it."

"Are you volunteering as the murderer, Uncle?"

"Just saying my piece. Coming clean. What I've realized this weekend is that due to accident of birth, one spends all one's life with a certain number of people without ever really liking any of them much."

"Thanks," said Roberts.

"Nice of you," said Clifford.

"Did you murder them?" asked Arlington.

"No."

"Then your breast-beating and general insults are unnecessary and irrelevent."

"I think my nephew did."

Everyone looked at Clifford. Who laughed.

"I did?"

Everyone had soup. No one was eating.

"You killed Huttenbach because he was a married man diddling your sister. You killed Lauderdale because he was a silly old man who married your mother. You killed Ashley because he was diddling the family finances, and you knew it. I had told you so. In my opinion, Ernie, during your recent tour of duty, you snapped somehow. You were under heavy fire, weren't you? It's happened before. When you see so much useless, sudden death . . ."

"One thing is certain," Arlington added. "Whoever killed Lauderdale and Ashley was physically strong. Clifford is strong."

"Strong or obsessed," D'Esopo said quietly.

"I'm strong for my age." Oland flexed his left arm. "Remarkably strong. Wiry. I never fail to do my exercises. A cold shower every morning of my life —"

"Arlington's the crazy one!" Clifford sputtered. "For God's sake, we all know that! He's been in and out of institutions more than —"

"Once!" Arlington shouted. "Years ago!"

Clifford jerked his thumb at his table mate. "He was damn near lobotomized."

Flynn's soup was warm.

"Years ago," Roberts said.

"Okay," Clifford yelled. "You think he hasn't been under pressure in Washington? Under pressure from us? What about all those real estate deals he's been making for himself in Canada? Talk about an obsessed personality!"

"I won't hear this talk!" Arlington slammed his fist on the table. "You all know me. I'm disgusted by your antics! Not one of you big, tough guys can get through a day without slaughtering some animal, shooting some helpless deer, holding a wriggling, suffocating fish up by its mouth! You guys can't live a day without bullying someone!"

" 'Bullying?' " Buckingham asked drily.

"Yes, bullying. Bullying me! Bullying Ashley!"

Thoughtfully, Roberts said, "Lauderdale was our best hunter. He never went out with rod or gun that he didn't —"

174

"And Huttenbach was the sloppiest," groaned Buckingham.

"And Uncle Buck's the biggest bully."

To Flynn, all these cross-accusations seemed another dinner-time game being played out.

The beer keg was being ignored.

"Why don't we all calm down," Roberts said in his committee-chairman voice. He smiled down the table at Eddy D'Esopo. "We all know each other pretty well. Very well, indeed. Something very different has been happening here these last few days. Something that hasn't happened in a hundred years at The Rod and Gun Club. Every few hours, someone is getting killed. Murdered. If you stand back and look at the situation, ask yourself what new, different element has been introduced to the club the last few days....?"

"Like a chemical formula," said Oland. "What new element has been added to bring about such radical change?"

"D'Esopo," said Clifford.

"Who *is* D'Esopo?" Roberts asked.

Chairs of the slain either side of him empty, D'Esopo looked large and isolated at his end of the table.

"I'm the Commissioner of Police for the City of Boston," D'Esopo said simply. "I'm a cop."

"Does anyone know D'Esopo?" Roberts asked. "I never saw him before in my life."

"He's not a member," said Arlington. "He's a guest."

"Whose guest?" Roberts asked. "Why?"

"I am— I was a guest of Mister Thomas Ashley. This is my third visit to The Rod and Gun Club."

"He came back this time to kill us all," Arlington said.

"Does anyone here really know D'Esopo?" asked Roberts.

Arlington looked myopically down the table. "The people who knew him best are all dead."

"There is the resentment factor," Clifford said. "We've all had to live with that."

"Which is why The Rod and Gun Club exists," Buckingham said. "To get away from damned fools and—"

"—cops," said Clifford. "People who feel the need to make middle-class judgements."

175

"Who knows more about how to murder people than a cop?" Arlington asked. "And who's quicker to make half-baked moral judgements?"

"I know about murdering people," Oland said. Only he and Flynn had emptied their soup bowls. "I'm quite good at it. You see, once you start thinking about your own death. . . ." Again his voice trailed off.

Clifford giggled. "Oland's killing off all his old friends so they'll be waiting for him in that great steam-room in the sky, Valhalla."

Taylor's head came around the swing door to the kitchen. He saw that most of the soup bowls still had soup in them and withdrew.

Buckingham nodded. "D'Esopo is the unknown element here. The different element."

"And," Roberts announced. "Apparently he was the one who got this . . . Flynn up here to investigate. A few minutes ago, in his room, Flynn told me that he is not investigating."

Quite seriously, Clifford asked, "Were you brought here not to investigate? Was that part of the understanding?"

"Instead he seems to be developing all sorts of material for blackmail," Roberts said. "In his room just now, he came out with quite a bill of particulars. For example, somehow he knows Arlington was confined at one point in his life —"

"God," said Buckingham. "He knows we've been flogging bodies around —"

"How much do you want?" Arlington demanded of Flynn.

"And there's Concannon, too," Clifford said.

"We've been set up!" concluded Arlington. "That's what happened. We've been set up! Someone was let into the club as guest, this D'Esopo, without being properly vetted, and now we've got three cops at table, a conspiracy if I ever saw one . . ."

"Three different methods of murder," Clifford said quietly.

Flynn said, "An entrancing idea. Is this why I was especially invited to dinner? To hear this?"

D'Esopo pushed his untasted soup away with his thumb. "If you want to know what a cop thinks, what one cop thinks. . . ." No one took him up on it. Everyone was silent. ". . . Well, all

176

this reminds me of indirect murder. Third-party murder. Where someone decides who dies and someone else actually does the murders."

"You mean, like in a mob, or a gang?" Clifford asked.

"Something like that." D'Esopo spoke diffidently. "I see two brains here."

Cocky was looking at the commissioner with interest.

"I think one guy is sitting back and keeping his nose clean..." D'Esopo continued slowly "...and the other guy is loyally following orders, doing what he's told whenever, however he can."

At the word *loyally*, first Clifford, then Arlington, then the rest looked at Wahler.

"And what would Mister Rutledge's motivation be?" Wahler asked in the tone of a detached lawyer.

"Maybe he knows something we don't know," said Buckingham.

"Or is thinking something we're not thinking," said Arlington.

"Your motive would be money," said Roberts. "Money and power. That's clear enough."

" 'Fraid you'll have to do better than that, gentlemen." Wahler said. "Your approaches to the problem may satisfy you, but the cats are still screaming in the trees."

In a quiet tone, Roberts asked, "Where is Rutledge, Wahler?"

"He wasn't even in the sauna," Buckingham said. "He rarely misses the sauna."

Roberts said: "Wahler. Go get Rutledge."

The silence around the table indicated concurrence.

Wahler left the room.

"You don't think I'm capable of doing murder?" Absently Oland rubbed his bare chest with his right hand and looked around the dining room. "Sometimes one gets tired of certain things, certain people, finally wants things his own way..."

"Wahler's the bastard," Clifford said. "All by himself. As sure as God made little green apples."

"He may well be," agreed Buckingham.

177

"Was he ever put up for membership?" Roberts asked.

"Yes and no," Buckingham answered. "Rutledge said the bastard's had the impertinence to suggest it. Several times."

"And what happened?" Roberts asked.

"Rutledge put him off."

"The point is," continued Oland, "murder is a social device, like any other."

Eyes smiling, Clifford said across the table to Flynn: "At least he's forgotten about his waterproofs."

Everyone looked at Wahler, standing in the door. "Rutledge's door is locked. He doesn't answer."

Cocky looked at Flynn for instructions about the key.

Flynn shook his head.

Roberts said, "Break the door down."

At the door to the dining room, Wahler hesitated.

Buckingham, clearly the most successful football lineman at the table, pushed his chair back. D'Esopo too, rose.

Wahler, Buckingham and D'Esopo left the room.

Clifford said to those remaining at the table, "My Uncle Buck loves to tease me. He always has. What he was really doing was clearing the air of charges against both him and me."

"I see," Cocky said.

Roberts asked Clifford, "Why didn't you go help break the door down? I should think that would be something a kid your age would want to do."

"Why didn't you?"

From upstairs, faintly, Flynn heard a door banged in its frame. Then a louder bang, and a louder. It was a strong door. Finally the splintering of wood and one final bang as the door bounced against a wall.

A few seconds of silence.

A deep, incomprehensible yell.

Everyone at the table remained at the table.

Dunn Roberts lowered his head.

"Dinner seems awfully slow tonight," Oland said in a peculiarly loud voice. "Wasn't cook ready?"

After another silent moment, Oland petulantly asked Flynn: "When is dinner coming in?"

"That's always the question, isn't it?"

Wahler was in the doorway then. "Rutledge is dead." He leaned one shoulder against the door frame. "Stabbed. The knife . . . ."

Next to Flynn, Oland gasped. His right hand never made it to his chest.

The naked old man's head fell forward into his empty soup bowl.

The bowl cracked.

His skinny shoulders sagged onto the table.

Flynn put out a hand to catch him.

Oland fell no further.

Across the table, Arlington shrieked. His eyes were round, staring at Oland's empty, cracked soup bowl.

Taking in breath, Arlington pushed his own soup bowl away, violently, making the soup in it slop out onto the table cloth. "We're being poisoned!"

Gracefully, Clifford had come around the table. With Roberts help, he lowered Oland to the floor and began cardio-pulmonary resuscitation.

"Poisoned!" yelled Arlington. "It's the Goddamned people in the kitchen! I knew it!"

Taylor came through the swing door from the kitchen carrying a roasted turkey on a carving tray.

He saw Clifford working over Oland's naked, bluing body on the floor.

The turkey skidded off the tray and bounced along the floor. Stuffing dropped out between the turkey's legs.

Passing Wahler in the doorway, Buckingham entered the dining room, and stopped. "What happened to Oland?"

"Poisoned!" Arlington shrieked. "He ate the soup! We're all being poisoned!"

"Heart attack, I suspect," said Flynn. "I ate the soup."

"Oh, God." Taylor said with dismay. "Another body to dispose of."

"Well." Flynn put his napkin beside his empty soup bowl. "There are dinner parties." He rose from his place at the table. "And there are dinner parties."

179

35

"**I** think I've got it."

"Cocky! Good man! I knew you'd crack this case!" Flynn steered a wide dinner tray through the door of his bedroom. "More to the immediate point, I've got victuals." On the tray were thick turkey sandwiches, a large pot of tea, cups and saucers.

From his seat at the chessboard, folders in his lap, Cocky asked, "Last time I saw that turkey, wasn't it behaving like a practice football?"

"Question not the source of your sustenance," Flynn said putting the tray on the floor beside the chess table, "and you might not starve." He handed a sandwich to Cocky. "Actually, I discovered I know one of the kitchen help. Our paths crossed previously in Afghanistan. At the time he was peddling passports."

"Always nice to know someone in the kitchen." Gladly Cocky bit into his sandwich.

"In most cases, it's essential." Flynn poured tea for them both, and helped himself to a sandwich. "Or so I have had every reason to observe."

Settled at his own side of the chess set, Flynn took a soiled envelope from his jacket pocket and handed it to Cocky. "Also a mash note for you. Taylor asked me to deliver it."

Putting down his tea cup, Cocky unfolded the note flat against the table. He read it, smiled, and handed it to Flynn.

It was handwritten in a big scrawl, apparently with a pencil stub.

"CORKY — COME OVER TO MY CABIN ABOUT TEN THIRTY FOR A DRINK, BRING YOU FREN FLIN — HEWITT

"Nice of him." Flynn dropped the note on Cocky's pile of folders. "Not sure I'll want to go out again in this weather."

"So what else is going on downstairs?" Cocky asked as he munched. "Any new corpses in the last half hour?"

"None reported to me. Now to the serious matter at hand."

On the chessboard, Flynn moved his Queen Rook to Queen One. "Roberts has been given the job of quickly driving Oland home, before he cools, and putting him in his own bed. It will be discovered in the morning, as the plan goes, that Oland died of a massive coronary occlusion while otherwise sleeping peacefully. I'm certain that, once again, The Rod and Gun Club will escape being mentioned in an obituary."

Cocky's Knight took Flynn's. "Senator Dunn Roberts is driving cross-country in a snow storm with a corpse propped up beside him? Supposing he gets stopped?"

"Wendell Oland was a gentleman of notably quiet manners." Flynn took Cocky's Knight with a Pawn.

"Did they dress him for the journey?"

"Hat, overcoat, and — he would have been pleased had he known — his new waterproofs."

"Still, he would regret the buckshot holes in them."

"Underneath all, a pair of pajamas so he can be popped into bed immediately upon his arriving home."

"They think of everything."

"Is Roberts our culprit?"

"Yes." Cocky put down his sandwich. His Rook took Flynn's. "And how are they disposing of Rutledge?"

And Flynn's Rook took Cocky's. "That they didn't confide in me. But I'm prepared to hear more bumps in the night."

"As long as they have some way of passing the time between dinner and bed. Right?"

Flynn began his second sandwich. "What makes Roberts the culprit?"

"Downstairs, in an alcove of the vault, is an ancient log book." Having the use of only his right hand, Cocky had to manipulate his sandwich, his cup of tea and his chess playing in turns. "After I returned to the vault with my satchel, I looked in the log book, just to see what the most recent entries were. Entries are made fairly regularly — there were about four last week. The most recent entry was on Saturday."

"The day the murders started."

"Concerning Senator Dunn Roberts." Cocky moved his Queen to Queen Seven and then reached for a folder he had

181

dropped on the floor. "Naturally, I assumed it was more housemaid gossip, regarding whose son failed trigonometry last term, or whatever."

Flynn moved his Queen to King Seven.

Cocky lifted two pieces of paper from the back of the folder. "This entry is a bit more serious." He handed one piece of paper to Flynn. "This is Dunn Roberts' voting record, with dates, as chairman of the Senate Transportation Deregulation Committee. You see, in each case he voted for deregulation." Cocky then handed Flynn the second piece of paper. "This is a summary of his wife's bank account over the last two years. Within twenty days of each deregulation vote, Mrs. Roberts's account benefitted from a sizable deposit."

"Source?"

"Not recorded."

"Sizable deposits indeed. Evidence suggests that either Senator Roberts has been accepting bribes, or that his wife is the agreed-upon heiress of a large family that has been dying like flies. How do these boyos keep thinking they can get away with it?"

Reaching, Flynn slid the papers back into the folder.

"Because they keep protecting each other, Frank."

"As long as they get to continue using each other."

"This vault system can only work by the honor method, Frank." Cocky moved his Rook to Queen Bishop One. "For example: I put something new in your file. To notify the rest of the members I have done so, I note the entry in the log book. Everyone else gets to look, but—"

"—I, the victim, possibly maligned, do not."

"Exactly."

"Or, if I do look, I shut up about it, do not protest, argue, or try to correct the file. I take it on the chin."

"Murdering off his fellow members is an almost secondary matter. My theory is that Senator Dunn Roberts broke Club rules. Saturday, he looked in his own file and saw what had just been entered against him."

"As he probably had a pretty good idea of what the entry was about."

Twisting in his chair to do so, Cocky picked a second sandwich from the tray. "He couldn't remove the entry until he was sure that everyone who had possibly read it had also been removed. Was dead."

"So he began killing off whoever had filed the evidence against him in the first place."

"But he let Walter March and Caxton Wheeler escape. They, too, could have read the entry."

"Both left suddenly." Cocky was enjoying his second sandwich as much as his first. "Wheeler by car at dawn, March by helicopter. No doubt Roberts figured he could get to them later. It was better for him to stay where most of the people were, and dispose of them one by one."

"Especially as they'd all be so cooperative in helping dispose of each other's bodies."

Cocky had to put down his sandwich to move his Rook to Queen Bishop One.

"But Cocky, old lad, sooner or later the last one left standing at The Rod and Gun Club would have to explain these murders, wouldn't he?"

"What murders? Huttenbach shot himself. Lauderdale was trampled by a horse. Ashley died in a car crash. Oland died at home in bed — or will do so as soon as he gets home to bed."

Flynn moved his Bishop to Knight Three. "The presumption is that members of the club who are not present know what's going on here, have been informed and been advising by telephone."

"But, Frank, do we know that to be so? Or has that been just one more device to intimidate us?"

"It has been repeated to us so often, I have been inclined to disbelieve it. My experience is that only lies need repeating."

Cocky moved his Pawn to King Rook Four. "I'm sure that Senator Dunn Roberts ultimately is up to reporting that a berserk member of the kitchen help is proven to be the culprit and, of course —"

"— has been quietly disposed of —"

"— again, as always —"

"— to preserve the privacy of The Rod and Gun Club."

Flynn moved his Queen to King Three. "Brilliant, Cocky! Absolutely brilliant! A good job of work!"

"I don't see that there is any other answer." Cocky placed his Queen on Queen Knight Seven.

Flynn glanced at his watch. "If you're right, if our murderer is Roberts, there's not much we can do about it at the moment, as our Senator is driving a corpse over hill and dale through a snowstorm. It's not yet nine thirty. But, if what you say is true, he will be back." Flynn moved his Queen to Bishop One. "I trust you noticed, Cocky, that during this evening's dinnertime game, everyone accused everyone else —"

"— but no one accused Dunn Roberts."

"And when it came Dunn Roberts's turn, cleverly he shifted the accusations to the outsider, our esteemed Commissioner Eddy D'Esopo. More tea? What a villain!"

"And it was Dunn Roberts who made Wahler go discover Rutledge's body."

"Suggesting Dunn Roberts knew Rutledge was dead. I think you've caught yourself a real villain here, Cocky, ol' lad."

Cocky took Flynn's Bishop Pawn with his Queen.

"But, Cocky, frankly your brilliant, practical solution rather frustrated my thoughtful, philosophical bent." Flynn's Queen took Cocky's Queen.

"Frank, even I have moments of impatience, if not intolerance, of your philosophical bent."

"I've been taken with the theory that the murders at The Rod and Gun Club have been being accomplished by an outsider."

"I know. That's why you drove me to Bellingham. That's why you interviewed Carl Morris, Carol Huttenbach, stopped at that tavern."

"The Three Belles of Bellingham. I'm sure those ladies would be pleased if they knew how much I've thought of them in this monastic environment." Flynn drained his tea cup. "It's just that elite groups are so seldom attacked successfully from within."

"Who else is there? Commissioner D'Esopo." Cocky took Flynn's Queen with his Rook. "Paul Wahler."

"Yes. Wahler." Flynn leaned over the chessboard. "Now that Rutledge is dead. Clearly, Wahler could want Rutledge's death to appear as one of several murders seeking a more general than specific solution. Wahler is executor of Rutledge's business affairs, and doubtlessly could profit heavily from Rutledge's death. And having been rejected by the membership, he has no real reason to protect the privacy, or secrecy, of The Rod and Gun Club. In fact, I suspect he'd rather enjoy turning the old place inside out."

"Taylor?"

"I've considered each possibility . . ." Flynn moved his King to Bishop Two. "Tell me, Cocky ol' lad. You've been to his cabin. For what does Hewitt need kerosene?"

In surprise, Cocky studied the chessboard.

In greater surprise, Cocky then studied Flynn's face.

"Hewitt's cabin has electricity," Cocky said. "An electric stove. Lights. Heat. The cabin has baseboard radiators."

"That was a damned good game of chess. I'm surprised I won." Flynn arose from the chessboard. "Seeing the weather's so inclement, I suggest we start a little early for Hewitt's cabin."

36

"I needn't remind you," Flynn said in a voice softened even more by the snow, "Hewitt is a professional hunter. He cannot speak, but he can see and he can hear. He knows these woods better than you know The Old Records Building on Craigie Lane. If he comes through the door of his cabin and sees any shape against the snowscape other than the rocks and trees he knows so well, hears any sound—"

"I know, Frank, I know."

Flynn was hunched over behind the boulder. He was sure Cocky, even standing erect, could not be seen from Hewitt's lit cabin.

"Cold?" Flynn asked.

"Just my feet."

"Sorry we couldn't take the time to outfit you with a proper pair of boots."

Flynn had insisted Cocky wear Flynn's overcoat over his own. As a result, Cocky looked rather like a short, round bear. Flynn wore the borrowed hunting jacket.

To avoid laying down a direct visible track in the snow, they had taken a circuitous route from the clubhouse to Hewitt's cabin. Walking through calf-high snow in two overcoats, partially paralyzed in his left side anyway, Cocky had progressed only by refining a lunging-ahead motion, a vertical sidestroke led by his right shoulder and right leg.

"Simply," Flynn said, "it occurred to me your friend, Hewitt, wanted you and me away from the main clubhouse shortly after ten o'clock."

"And he had gotten a big supply of kerosene from the kitchen." They had been standing still long enough in the woods so that Cocky's outer overcoat and Flynn's borrowed hunting jacket were whitened by the falling snow. "Why didn't I think!"

"At least, I'm glad it came up in conversation."

"Hewitt was in the storeroom." Cocky's voice was low, devoid of inflection. "Huttenbach, healthy, spoiled man, sloppy

186

hunter, came in, probably walked right by Hewitt without seeing him, hearing him. And Hewitt just picked up one of the shotguns that was there, loaded it, and blasted him."

"Probably impulsively. But after years and years of wanting to do some such thing."

In the black and white world of the snowy wood, Flynn remembered the speechless sadness in Hewitt's face looking up from the twisted corpse of the doe which had broken her neck against the electrified fence. What had that fence meant to Hewitt? The decades of wild, loud, drunken, careless slaughter of fish and game within that fence; the endless, indifferent ability to restock the fish and game; the senseless despoilation of the forest?

"Lauderdale in an evening gown is sitting shrieking at the piano," Cocky continued, "and Hewitt, who cannot speak at all, comes through the window behind him, maybe with a piece of rope which just happened to be in his pocket, and throttles him."

"A dying man," Flynn said. "He had nothing to lose. And he had something to say. And no other way of saying it."

"Hunting out by the Rumble de Dump, he just walks up behind Ashley and bashes his skull in with a tree branch."

"And I left Hewitt to guard the body," Flynn chuckled. "Score one for me. We think of the Hewitts of this world as the salt of the earth."

"Frank, think of the shit he's had to listen to, for years, on these hunting and fishing trips. They knew they could say anything they wanted in front of Hewitt. He couldn't repeat it. Big talk. Mean talk. Nasty talk. Drunken talk. The secret characteristics and foibles of each other and of others who run the world."

"We kill all the deer!

"And drink all the beer!

"Live without fear!

"Sure no one can hear!" quoted Flynn.

"Hewitt could hear. Everything. Years and years of everything. And they were destroying the world he cared for. He goes to Rutledge's room with a hunting knife —"

The lights in the cabin went out.

187

"He's accustoming his eyes to the darkness before coming out," Flynn said. "Hewitt's not the urban-type hunter you're used to, Cocky. Once that door opens, do not move a muscle."

"Not by half," Cocky muttered.

The center of the cabin wall grew darker. The door had opened.

All around them the landing snow hissed.

Only vaguely could Hewitt's silhouette be seen against the cabin wall.

As he stepped out from the cabin and became silhouetted by the snow it became clear that under his right arm Hewitt carried a long gun. What looked like a paint bucket swung from his left hand.

"That the kerosene?" Flynn whispered.

"Yes."

"Okay," Flynn said softly after Hewitt had walked into the line of trees nearer the dirt road. "If you follow me, Cocky, follow at a good distance."

"Can't keep up with you anyway."

"And, by the way, Cocky: I suspect ol' Hewitt himself would advise you not to get into that straight line between himself and his cabin."

Flynn left Cocky behind the boulders.

Following a course parallel to Hewitt, well behind him, Flynn kept to the woods outside the cabin's clearing. Walking, Flynn did not pick up his feet much, but pushed them along under the snow. The toes of his boots stopped at rocks and roots without tripping him.

In the woods near the road, Flynn waited. Standing stock still behind a tree, he watched Hewitt come down the road. He walked through the snow as a city person would along a sidewalk in June.

It was a shotgun Hewitt was carrying.

After passing Flynn, down the road, nearer the clubhouse, Hewitt stopped. He looked around. Obviously he had found Flynn's and Cocky's tracks crossing the road on their way to his cabin. Flynn supposed Hewitt was trying to guess from the amount of new snow that had fallen in the tracks how much time had passed since the tracks were fresh.

Hewitt hesitated a long moment, looking around, listening. Then he went on.

Flynn decided he had seen enough, knew enough to pursue Hewitt openly, confront him. In the dark of the night the man was headed for the clubhouse with a shotgun and a bucket of kerosene.

By the time Flynn had scrambled through the snow-filled, rocky ditch onto the road, Hewitt had disappeared.

"Hewitt!" Flynn bellowed.

Hurrying now, Flynn ran down the road following Hewitt's tracks.

The tracks went off the road, to the left, across a ditch and into the woods. The path wandered uphill through the woods.

Halfway up the hill, Flynn stumbled. He landed on his hands and knees. He raised his head and yelled, "Hewitt!" He realized Hewitt could think Flynn was calling for him down at his cabin.

When he stood up, Flynn broke into as much of a run as he could manage up the rest of the path.

He found himself at the back of the clubhouse, facing the back porch. The lights in the kitchen were off.

On the porch, something struck the gong, just lightly, just touched it. Nevertheless, it made a noise.

Someone crouching beside the gong stood up.

Flynn ran toward the back of the house.

Hewitt was swinging the bucket, throwing kerosene widely over the back wall of the porch.

Hearing Flynn, he turned around, dropped the bucket. He picked the shotgun up from where it leaned against the gong.

In a rush Hewitt came down the few stairs of the porch. He carried the shotgun at an angle high across his chest. He looked like a canoeist changing his paddle from one side of the boat to another.

Slipping in the snow, Flynn raised his left arm to catch the blow. Flynn yelled, loud, twice.

Nothing hit his left arm.

The shotgun stock cracked against the side of his head, just above his left ear.

Falling, Flynn thought how nice the snow would feel against his face.

He never felt it.

First he heard the flames. Then many excited Vietnamese shouting orders.

Someone was holding him in a sitting position in the snow, facing away from the clubhouse. A warm hand was on the back of his neck.

Flickering light from the flames were turning the snow around Flynn red, yellow.

Brown, thin bare legs, bare feet were in the snow beside him.

A high voice asked, "You okay?"

Flynn nodded his head and regretted the pain. "I'm okay."

The hand left his neck. The bare feet flew from the snow like two little birds.

Flynn looked around from where he was seated in the snow.

A half dozen agile Vietnamese, the kitchen help, bare arms and feet flashing warmly in the firelight against the snow, were scooping up armfuls of snow and throwing it at the fire. Flames were climbing the back walls of the porch curling up the struts holding up the roof. Smoke billowed out from under the roof. Now the lights were on in the kitchen, the kitchen door open. The flames were moving fast over the old timber, but the Vietnamese were moving even faster.

While Flynn watched, one side of the gong's smouldering oak frame collapsed. Like a huge discus, the gong fell to the floor of the porch with a sour clunk. Its own weight caused it to roll slowly off the porch. It dragged its frame with it into the snow.

The Vietnamese cheered.

The kitchen help seemed to be making rather a party of the

190

fire. Barefooted in the snow, their movements made a pretty dance.

Their job was greatly aided by the collapse of the porch roof. The snow on the roof helped smother the fire.

Hands in the snow, Flynn pushed himself into a kneeling position. Another concentrated push and he was standing in the snow. He swayed slightly.

For a moment he felt nauseous. His fingers felt the bump over his left ear. He watched the Vietnamese working on the edges of the fire. A kitchen window was smoked, cracked.

Then he started down the hill, going off the path, to the right, following Hewitt's tracks.

Of course Flynn could not move fast over rough ground downhill through the snow. What he wanted was to breathe deeply, evenly through his nose. What he really wanted was to lie down in the snow.

And he was not thinking about what he was doing with great clarity. He had been following Hewitt before he was cracked on the head. He had gotten up and begun following Hewitt again.

When he came to the dirt road it took him a moment to figure out what he was seeing. In the middle of the road, he turned in a slow circle.

Hewitt's tracks went to the right along the road, in as straight a line as the road permitted, to the right of the tracks he had made coming from his cabin.

A very messy track came onto the road from the ditch the other side, made a wide curve in the road and, not going in a straight line at all, followed Hewitt's tracks.

The two tracks together made it seem that something as efficient as a cross-country skier was being pursued by something as inefficient as a donkey-powered plow.

Cocky was following Hewitt.

Hewitt had murdered Huttenbach, Lauderdale, Ashley and Rutledge. He had tried to kill everyone, except Cocky and Flynn.

191

Hewitt was carrying a shotgun, and was expert at using it. He had hunted these woods professionally for decades.

Flynn ran a few steps following the tracks. The pounding in his head slowed him to a walk. It warned him of renewed unconsciousness. He moved at the fastest parade march of which he was capable.

Hewitt's tracks went off the road, across the ditch, and into the dark woods. On the right-hand side of the road. On the opposite side of the road from his cabin.

Hewitt knew he was being followed.

Cocky's churned-up track also left the road. A wide, circular area of snow in the ditch was messed up. Cocky must have fallen, struggled in the snow, gotten himself up. His track led up the other side of the ditch, into the wood.

Flynn raised his eyes, up into the dark trees. Many still had late foliage on them. This was an early snow, for these woods. Two thousand acres of trees, and Hewitt knew every square meter.

Strong-hearted Cocky, with no experience Flynn knew of, off the city streets, was following Hewitt, dragging after an armed, professional hunter, in the dark, in the snow, in the hunter's own woods.

Head down again, Flynn went through the ditch. He followed Cocky's more erratic trail.

Well into the woods, head throbbing, tired himself, Flynn stopped. He had just climbed a rise. Before him was a fairly open area.

Hewitt's clean tracks went somewhat to the right.

Cocky's ever-thickening track crossed Hewitt's oddly, and went to the left.

Many meters ahead of Flynn was a tall, dark, thick tree, leaves still on it, almost a structure by itself, looking solid, sheltering.

Puffs of steam were coming from the side of the tree.

In the snowing, dark night of the woods, Flynn focused his eyes on the tree.

Cocky was leaning his back against the tree, head bowed, breathing hard.

192

Before Flynn could move to him, Cocky said, "Hewitt...."

Cocky's white face became visible against the dark tree trunk. "Hewitt!"

Flynn decided to stand easy, to wait. To see what would happen. If Hewitt had wanted to rid himself of Cocky, it would have been easy enough to shoot him by now.

"I can't chase you any more," Cocky said to the stark wood. "I'm a crippled man. You know that."

The only response was the hiss of the snow.

In a conversational tone, as if Hewitt were standing beside him, Cocky said, "I can't catch you." Flynn watched Cocky shake his head. "You're old and you're sick, you're dying, Hewitt, but you're a professional hunter, you know these woods, you probably even know how to get out of them, through the fence, and you've got a gun, and...I can't catch you. I can't come after you any more."

Flynn pressed gloved fingers against the bump over his ear. He breathed deeply, as silently as he could.

"You killed a lot of people, Hewitt. Murdered 'em. Young Huttenbach, and crazy old Lauderdale, and that nervous jerk, Ashley. That pompous Rutledge. You gotta get caught, Hewitt. We've got to make sure you're stopped. You know that."

The next pause was long.

Flynn was about to step forward when Cocky said, "I can't catch you, man!"

Flynn waited another moment.

The right corner of his eye detected a small movement across the clearing from Cocky. Someone was moving.

Then this dark form moved steadily through the trees toward Cocky.

It was Hewitt.

And he was carrying his shotgun in the crook of his arm, in no position to be fired.

Flynn remained silent, still, in the hissing wood.

Hewitt's gait was not all that certain. As he crossed the snowfield, his body was bent, his legs wobbly. At one point he stopped and took a deep breath.

Finally he stopped within the reach of Cocky under the big tree.

Hewitt held out the shotgun to Cocky, for Cocky to take.

Cocky pushed himself off the tree. He stood as erect as he could. He waved away the shotgun. "I can't carry it," he said. "I'll have all I can do to get myself back."

Cocky began to lurch through the snow. He fell.

Behind him, Hewitt dropped to his knees silently in the snow. He put down his shotgun. He held onto his stomach with both hands. He doubled over.

Floundering tiredly, trying to straighten himself in the snow, to stand up, Cocky did not look around at Hewitt. He did not see that Hewitt, too, had fallen.

In the still, stark wood in a dark, snowing night, silently Flynn watched two men struggling quietly with their own mortality, their mortification, their pride, victims of their own experiences, their humanity, their handicaps, their dignities, their beliefs, prisoners of each other, of their own lives, of damaged bodies and believing minds, in fresh and still-falling snow.

By the time Cocky had regained his feet, behind him, Hewitt, too, had stood with his shotgun under his arm and taken deep and, Flynn was sure, painful breath.

With his free hand, then, Hewitt took Cocky's arm.

"I can walk," Cocky said. He lurched forward and almost fell again. "It's just that my shoes are so wet."

The hunter and the hunted passed the silent Flynn in the wood. Neither saw him nor heard him there.

Struggling along courageously, back to their more certain futures, took all their combined efforts, all their concentrations.

194

37

"**G**ood morning, Grover. Are you there at all?"

It was shortly after nine Tuesday morning. Flynn's head still hurt, still had a considerable knob over the left ear, but he had slept with the help of aspirin, arisen somewhat refreshed, bathed, packed, enjoyed the tea and toast Taylor had delivered without being asked.

Outside bright sun poured from a clear sky onto the fresh snow.

And the telephone worked.

"I'm here, Inspector."

"Tell me, Grover, did you get an urgent message yesterday to telephone me?"

"Yes."

"And you got the number to call?"

"Yes."

"And did you try to call me?"

"No."

"You didn't. Why not?"

"Because I knew the source of the call, Inspector."

"I was the source of the request."

"Stacey Matson called me, Mrs. Willard Matson, crying like a loon into the phone saying I had to call you right away."

"You don't observe the requests of weeping women?"

"We have her husband in custody, Inspector. For hit-and-run. For the killing of Hiram Goldberg."

"I needed you to call me, Grover."

"Yeah, and I know about what. A crying woman, the wife of a felon, calls you, wherever the hell you are, tells you some big sob story. How did she know where to call you? I didn't."

"A coincidence, Grover. She had the wit to call my house. Her call was passed on to me here."

"Yeah, well, she must be a pretty good friend to be calling your home."

195

"She has met my wife. They serve on some committee. The Committee to Encourage Young People to Play Together, or some such thing."

"You told this Matson dame to call me."

"Yes. I was unable to do so myself."

"I had just arrested her husband, Frank."

"One thing did not have to do with the other."

"You told her to tell me to call you."

"I can see it might not seem like the best form, Grover, but under the circumstances —"

"And you were going to tell me to release the poor, weeping woman's husband. Right? He killed a guy, Frank."

"Among other things, I was going to tell you to investigate the possibility of child abuse in the Matson family. Before releasing the husband."

"Exactly. I knew all that. You try to run an investigation by telephone and then tell me I've made a bad arrest? I've had enough of all this, Frank."

"Mrs. Matson was my only way of getting a message to you."

"I bet. I checked the area code of the telephone number she gave me. You're in the mountains, Inspector. In the resort area. Hard at work playing chess with Concannon by the fire, Frank?"

"When you get a message to call me, Grover, under any circumstances —"

"I'm writing a full report to the Commissioner."

"You're what?"

"I've had it. Every week I request a transfer."

"Every week I request you to be transferred."

"Now I'm writing the Commissioner a letter telling him exactly why, Frank. The Commissioner personally."

"You mean, D'Esopo?"

"That's another thing. You're not supposed to call your superiors by their last names. He's Commissioner D'Esopo to you, Inspector."

"I stand corrected."

"Everything you do is bad for morale."

"Your morale."

"The morale of the whole police force. Like calling me Grover."

"It distinguishes you."

"Your sudden, unexplained disappearances. Like your present absence. And the fact that you keep getting away with it. I've kept a complete log. Dates, your excuses, everything. According to the records, you've had your appendix out twice, Frank."

"Healthy diet. I keep growing new ones."

"You keep me from bowling on the Police League. On Sunday night, for God's sake. I've been complimented by being put on the Eats Committee, and you won't even cooperate. You won't even tell me if you like tuna fish."

"About this Matson business, Grover, I'll be in the office this afternoon —"

"Trying to do your work by telephone, while you're off at some resort. Falling for stories any weeping women give you. I've had it! I'm putting it all down in black and white, Frank, you're a lousy police officer, and I'm sending the full report to Commissioner D'Esopo personally."

"It won't do you any good, Grover."

"I'd like to know why not."

Flynn decided he would say the most elitist thing he could think of before hanging up.

"Because," he said, "we know something you don't know."

●

38

When Flynn came out of his room, baggage in hand, Senator Dunn Roberts was loitering on the upper landing.

"Good morning, Inspector Flynn. How do you feel?"

"Like a man who has been drugged unconscious one night and knocked unconscious with the butt of a shotgun the next. Like a man who has been lied to, used, played with, insulted and imprisoned."

"Insulted?"

"I'm not forgetting being served broccoli, boiled fish and tapioca pudding at one sitting."

"Oh."

The door to Suite 23 was open.

"And what imaginative demise did you engineer for Charles Rutledge the Second?"

"You'll read about it in the newspapers."

"I'm sure. Been quite a rash of prominent men dying by accident in these environs lately."

"Well, they were all active men. Sportsmen."

"And what scheme have you hatched for the man Hewitt?"

Folding his arms across his chest, Roberts leaned his lower back against the banister. "Your friend, Concannon, has sat up with him all night, you know."

"It doesn't surprise me."

"He agrees with our plan. This morning, Buckingham and Taylor will drive Hewitt to a small hospital for incurables supported by the Huttenbach Foundation. And there, nature will take its course. He'd never live to stand trial, Flynn. There would be absolutely no point in your putting the wheels of justice into motion."

"There's justice, and there's justice." Flynn took a step closer to Roberts. "You're resigning from the United States Senate."

Roberts looked up in surprise. "I am?"

"Within thirty days."

"Why would I do that?"

"Because you have profited enough from your seat in the Senate. Especially has your wife's bank account swollen each time you have cast a vote in your Transportation Deregulation Committee." Flynn stepped back. "There's my reward."

Roberts studied Flynn's eyes. "You have some evidence?"

"Of course."

Roberts looked away. He stood up from the banister. He blinked, but only once. Then he said: "You're a gentleman, Flynn."

"But not," Flynn said, heading for the stairs, "a member of The Club."

Jacket collar up in the bright morning, Commissioner Eddy D'Esopo stood on the front porch of The Rod and Gun Club watching the slow-moving scene in front of him.

"How's your head?" he asked Flynn.

"Which one?"

In the parking lot, Hewitt was overseeing Taylor packing things in the trunk of a car. On the other side of the car, Buckingham was pacing up and down.

Nearby, Cocky stood, satchel in hand.

"You all right to drive?" D'Esopo asked.

"It's mostly downhill from here. You extending your stay at The Rod and Gun Club?"

"Going upstairs to pack now."

"Oh. Thought you might want to have another go at the locks on the refrigerator doors."

Hewitt was writing something on a piece of paper, using the car roof as a writing surface.

"I'm very grateful to you, Frank."

"You're very grateful to Detective Lieutenant Walter Concannon, Retired, Eddy. He's the one who brought the murderer in. Last night, you would have been burned to death in your bed, Eddy, if it hadn't been for Detective Lieutenant Walter Concannon. Retired."

D'Esopo nodded. "He's not retired any more. He'll be back on full pay before the end of the week, Frank."

Clifford was coming down the slope on cross-country skis.

"Retroactively reinstated, if you please," Flynn said. "Cocky never did retire, you know."

"Retroactively reinstated," D'Esopo agreed.

Across the driveway, Hewitt handed Cocky the piece of paper, folded.

"Anything I can do for you, Frank?"

For a moment, Flynn thought. He knew he would kick himself for not taking this opportunity to rid himself and his office, his life, of Sergeant Richard T. Whelan. But, at the moment, Flynn had the distinct desire to oppress Grover. If not oppress him, at least teach him to return telephone calls.

"No," Flynn said. "Nothing."

As Flynn crossed the driveway, Taylor backed the car out of its parking space.

Buckingham sat in the back seat with Hewitt.

Cocky stood clear of the car.

Clifford slid alongside Flynn on his skis and stopped.

Together, they watched the car go down the slope and move slowly along the road at the edge of the lake.

Clifford said: "Why did he hate us so much?"

Flynn turned and looked at Clifford hanging over the ski poles propped in his armpits. At his handsome tanned face, clear eyes against the bright snow, superbly cut, full black hair, broad shoulders in an expensive dark, handknit sweater, tall, slim body on the light skis. At a young man promoted well beyond his age and experience in a glamorous, powerful job. Bursting with health, more safe from the ravages of disease and accident than others. More safe from the law. Guaranteed, as much as one can be, a permanent, important place in the big world, a voice and the ability to use it.

Flynn said: "Have a nice ski, Ernest."

200

Scrub-A-Dub (West Bend)
1515 South Main Street
262-334-4759

Cashier2,   02/02/20, 12:43 PM
Shift 1, Empl 3729,   Sale # 60539646521

---

1 Xpress Wash   4.74

Subtotal   4.74
Sales Tax   0.26
Total   5.00

Cash   5.00

Car# 19

FREE $12 SUPERWASH TODAY!
With purchase of $25 or more GIFT CARD.

Cocky was in the front passenger seat of the Country Squire station wagon, boxed chess set beside him, satchel at his feet, when Flynn got behind the wheel. Flynn had put his own luggage in the back of the car.

Cocky sneezed.

"The heater will work in a minute," Flynn said, starting the car.

" 'Fraid I've got a bit of a cold."

Backing the car around, Flynn said, "We might just stop at the Three Belles of Bellingham. Pour some Jameson's whiskey into you. Isn't that good for a cold?"

"No." Cocky wiped his nose with a handkerchief. "But it would make me feel better."

He looked around at the huge, dark-timbered Rod and Gun Club as Flynn drove down the slope to the lake.

"It's a wonder that old place didn't burn down in a minute."

"Ach, Cocky. The elite are ever with us."

Snow sparkled along the roughly plowed road. To their right, sunlight shimmered on the lake. Overhead, snow lay along the dark branches of the trees.

"Mind my asking what was on that piece of paper Hewitt handed you?"

With the fingers of his right hand Cocky held up the note so Flynn could read it as he drove.

"Sily bastids think they run the wurld."

"Truth is," Flynn said. "They do."